THE EMPRESS'S DAGGER

THE EMPRESS'S DAGGER

TOUCHING TIME BOOK 2

AMANDA ROBERTS

Red Empress Publishing
www.RedEmpressPublishing.com

Copyright © Amanda Roberts
www.AmandaRobertsWrites.com

Cover by Cherith Vaughan
www.shreddedpotato.com

ALSO BY AMANDA ROBERTS

Fiction

Threads of Silk

The Man in the Dragon Mask

The Qing Dynasty Mysteries

Murder in the Forbidden City

Murder in the British Quarter

Murder at the Peking Opera

The Touching Time Series

The Emperor's Seal

The Empress's Dagger

The Slave's Necklace

Nonfiction

The Crazy Dumplings Cookbook

Crazy Dumplings II: Even Dumplinger

ONE

*T*he wind howled and waves crashed over the side of the ship, but Jiayi's footing was solid in her boots with thick tread. They had been awkward to move in at first—nothing like the precarious pot-bottom shoes she usually wore—but as the ship rocked back and forth, she was soon grateful for the heavy soles that seemed to anchor her to the deck.

Jiayi looked down at the saber in her hand, the one she was holding in real life as well, and admired the etchings in the steel of the blade. It was a gorgeous weapon, and she loved what happened when she gripped it.

She became Ching Shih, the pirate queen. She ruled from the South China Sea through the Sea of Japan and had a fleet of five hundred ships. Hundreds of thousands of men bent the knee to her and obeyed her every command.

But she could not revel in her power now. Her ship was launching an attack, and she had to do what the empress had sent her to do—find the map that led to Ching Shih's massive treasure hoard.

Jiayi climbed up on the deck railing, her saber in one

hand, a rope in the other. Despite the driving rain, the time for battle had come. She signaled to her helmsman, and he nodded as he spun the wheel, guiding her ship, the *Hongqi*, *Red Flag*, to pull alongside the *Mogui*, the *Devil*.

"Get ready, men," Jiayi yelled. "Lanshe did not just betray me, but all of us. Today, we get our revenge!"

The men—and women; Ching Shih accepted any person willing to fight for her—raised their voices and their swords, chanting her name and raining down curses on Lanshe, Blue Snake, Ching Shih's former first mate and lover. She had trusted him—too much. And now, she was going to rectify that mistake.

Jiayi wondered how long she had already been in the dream. It was almost impossible for her to keep track of time when she was having a vision. She knew that time traveled differently, usually more quickly, when she was in a dream, but she often only knew when she was about to wake up when her vision started to go black and she had trouble breathing. But so far, she had not felt any of the symptoms, even though she was certain she had already been Ching Shih for several minutes. She only hoped she could hang on long enough to find Lanshe and get what she came for.

The *Hongqi* sidled up to the *Mogui* and Jiayi yelled, giving the signal for the attack. She and her men used their ropes to swing over to the *Mogui*, where Lanshe's men were waiting for her, their own swords brandished.

Jiayi swung high to avoid the enemies waiting along the edge of the deck of the *Mogui*. She had to get to Lanshe as quickly as possible. As she hovered over the water below, her heart was in her nose. She couldn't believe what she was doing! It was terrifying and exhilarating at the same time. She let go of the rope and landed firmly on her feet on the deck of the *Mogui*. Two men charged at her, their swords raised and a curse on their lips, but Jiayi swung her sword low, surprising the men by injuring them both in the legs simultaneously. They crumpled to the ground. Jiayi could feel Ching Shih raise her saber to end their miserable lives, but she stayed the pirate's hand. She couldn't kill helpless men, even if they were murderous pirates who would end her life without a second thought. Ching Shih lowered her sword and ran around the fallen men, heading for the helm, where she knew Lanshe would be.

As she reached the top of the stairs to the helm, she saw Lanshe fighting several of her men who had managed to break through the line of pirates on the deck.

"Leave him!" Ching Shih ordered. "He is mine!"

Ching Shih's men immediately withdrew, rushing down the stairs back to the deck to help their fellow pirates. Lanshe turned to Ching Shih and his lips curled into a smile.

"Finally," he said. "You have hidden from me long enough."

"I never hide," she said. "You stole from me. You ran. You have no honor or courage. Give me the map—"

"And you will let me live?" he interrupted with a laugh. "How ladylike of you."

"A quick death," she clarified, a strike of lightning reflecting in her blade. "If I have to take the map from you, I'll take your tongue as a trophy as well."

Lanshe laughed with a toss of his head, but Jiayi knew it was false bravado. Lanshe had never bested Ching Shih in a sword fight, which was why he had been fleeing. He knew that if she ever caught him, he would be dead. She had been chasing him for months, and this was not their first battle. But it was the first in which they had come face to face, and they both knew they would never meet again—in this life at least.

Jiayi did not wait for Lanshe to ready himself before she ran at him. Over the years of falling into different bodies and fighting various forms of combat, she knew that pirates were among the least honorable in their fighting style. There was no polite dance or respect for customs. Pirates fought to the death, often desperately. That did not mean they had no skill. On the contrary, Ching Shih was one of the most skilled swordswomen Jiayi had ever come across. But she still fought with less form, fewer rules.

Lanshe jumped back, slashing in defense, knocking Jiayi's saber aside. But Jiayi didn't give up, and she didn't hold back. She was on the offensive, closing the gap Lanshe was desperate to keep between them. Jiayi licked at the salt on her lips from the sea air as she lunged toward Lanshe. The ship careened to the side, and Jiayi had to step back to keep her balance. Lanshe saw his opportunity to strike at Ching Shih and took it, running at her with his blade in front of him. He struck Ching Shih in the stomach and laughed, believing he had landed a fatal blow.

But Jiayi smiled back, and he quickly realized his error. He pulled his blade back, revealing that he had managed to tear a hole in her shirt—but not in the thin leather under-garments she wore as light armor.

He grunted as Jiayi ran her saber into his belly, then he collapsed at her feet, doing his best to keep his entrails from slipping onto the deck. Jiayi kicked him in the shoulder, sending him onto his back. She rummaged through his pockets until she found it—the crude map he had drawn revealing where she had hidden a large portion of her trea-sure hoard. The rain fell into her eyes and she did her best to interpret the map, but it wasn't exactly clear to her. She couldn't read and knew very little of geography.

"Where is it?" she screamed, kicking Lanshe in the ribs as he groaned in pain. Jiayi started a bit at the sights of the blood pooling around him and then quickly washed away by the water sloshing around the deck. She had killed this man. Even though Ching-shi had been the one to land the fatal blow hundreds of years ago, Jiayi had felt her sword slide into his stomach. His blood was on her hands. She tamped her feelings down. She had to find the treasure before it was too late.

"Don't you know?" Lanshe asked with a cough as blood sputtered from his mouth.

She kneeled down next to him and pointed at what looked to be an island circled in red. "What is this place?"

Lanshe reached up and touched her cheek. She could feel the warmth of the blood on his fingers. "The place... where...we met..." he said. Then he exhaled, the life fleeing his body.

Jiayi stood up and kicked the dead man. "Tell me!" she screamed, but he could not. She kneeled back down by his side and drew a dagger. She opened his mouth and gripped his tongue.

"I warned you..." she growled.

Jiayi didn't want to see what happened next.

She opened her eyes and saw the empress waiting for her anxiously.

"Well?" the empress prodded. "Did you see it?"

"I did," Jiayi said.

The empress laughed, the dry cackling sound devolving into a rough cough before she cleared her throat. "Where is it?" she asked. "Where is the treasure?"

"I'm sorry," Jiayi said. "I don't know the name of the place, not yet."

The empress stood upright and glared down at Jiayi. The empress was not a tall woman, but her presence was larger than any person Jiayi had ever met.

"What?" the empress snapped, her eyes narrow.

"I saw it, but I couldn't read the words," Jiayi explained. "And I didn't recognize the places..."

"Then go back!" the empress commanded, grabbing Jiayi's hands and squeezing them around the hilt of the saber.

"I...I can't!" Jiayi said. She had no idea when she would be able to have another vision, and even when she did, she couldn't guarantee that she would be back in the same place or time. She might never see the map again.

The empress grunted and slapped Jiayi across the face, as she usually did when she was frustrated with the girl, even though she knew that Jiayi's abilities were limited. "You are becoming more trouble than you are worth!" the empress spat.

"Now, now," Princess Der Ling said, stepping forward and gently helping Jiayi to stand, offering her a kerchief to wipe her mouth with. "I am sure that Jiayi saw something useful."

"I...I think so," Jiayi said, all the excitement of being Ching Shih having drained out of her. She wasn't a brave pirate queen—she was nothing more than a palace slave. She had to remember that. "I saw the map clearly, and I have a good memory. I could draw it, the islands and the characters. I am sure that Zhihao could then find out where the treasure is."

The empress sighed. "Fine," she said. "Get to work.

When you are done, go fetch Zhihao. I have something to discuss with him."

"Yes, Your Majesty," Jiayi said, kneeling.

"I'm tired," the empress declared, then she left the room for her sleeping quarters, her dozens of ladies and eunuchs following behind. Only Jiayi and Der Ling stayed behind.

"Thank you," Jiayi said as she fingered Der Ling's kerchief, keeping her eyes downcast.

"It was nothing," Der Ling said. "I can handle the old bat's moods."

Jiayi didn't respond. She didn't find Der Ling's confidence and irreverence humorous or reassuring. She adjusted her sleeves so that she was no longer holding the saber with her bare hands. She didn't think she would be able to have another vision for some time, but she didn't want to take the risk.

"What happened while you were in the vision?" Der Ling asked.

"I was Ching Shih," Jiayi said. "And I was fighting Lanshe—"

"No," Der Ling interrupted. "You were gone a long time."

"I was?" Jiayi asked, looking up.

Der Ling nodded. "Nearly ten minutes. I thought you had died."

Jiayi was surprised. She did not think she had ever been in a vision for that long before. She was usually only able to have a vision for as long as she was able to hold her breath. But now that she thought about it, she hadn't been panting or strangling when she woke up like she usually was. She also didn't black out when she was in the vision. She chose to wake up. Perhaps her meditation sessions with Hu

Xiaosheng were working to strengthen her abilities. But she only shook her head at Der Ling.

"I don't know," she said. "Everything seemed the same to me."

Der Ling pressed her lips as though she wasn't sure she believed Jiayi, but then she smiled. "Well, as long as you are safe."

Jiayi smiled back, but she hesitated to say much more. She wanted to trust Der Ling. She needed someone within the palace walls she could rely on. But Der Ling was a powerful woman. As the daughter of a diplomat and a foreigner, she was well-known and had many important connections. She also had the love of the empress. Most women as lowly as Jiayi would do anything to have a friend like Der Ling on her side. But such a friendship usually came at a great cost. Women like Der Ling did not befriend girls like Jiayi for nothing.

Der Ling then pulled the ornate dagger that had once belonged to Empress Wu out of her sleeve and offered it to Jiayi. Jiayi reached toward it, but she stopped. She could feel heat radiating from the dagger without even touching it.

"What is it?" Der Ling asked, her eyes wide.

"I don't know," Jiayi said. She could feel the dagger pulling at her, dragging her back into the world of her visions. But it wasn't possible for her to have another vision so soon...was it? And she'd never felt strange energy from an item, even the dagger, and she had touched the dagger before.

"What are you afraid of?" Der Ling asked.

"There is something strange about that dagger," Jiayi admitted. "I don't like it."

Der Ling laughed as she ran her finger along the

dagger's carved sheath. "Don't worry. I'm not afraid. Whatever this dagger has to teach us, I'm ready for it."

Jiayi couldn't help but shake her head. Der Ling had no idea what she was toying with. Jiayi had nearly died in her visions more times than she cared to remember.

"As soon as your strength returns," Der Ling said, "come to me so we can try again with the dagger. We are running out of time. We need to learn as much about Empress Wu as possible before the empress does."

"Yes, Your Highness," Jiayi said with a curtsey.

Der Ling turned and left, and Jiayi breathed a sigh of relief. She had agreed to help Der Ling understand the significance of Empress Wu's dagger, but she was now having second thoughts. It was difficult enough serving the empress, but now having to keep a secret from her and answer to Der Ling was becoming more than she could handle. The empress was obsessed with Empress Wu. If she found out that Jiayi and Der Ling had been hiding the dagger from her...Well, Der Ling would suffer no more than being sent home. But Jiayi shuddered to think of what the empress would do to her.

Jiayi looked around and realized she was alone. Usually, when the empress had Jiayi touch an item, she would take the item away when the vision was complete. But this time the empress had left the saber behind. Jiayi did her best to hide the saber in her sleeves as she crept back to her room. She would give the sword to Zhihao later. He would be thrilled to have an item that belonged to Ching Shih for his museum.

Back in her room, Jiayi placed the sword under the thin straw mattress of her bed, just to keep anyone from seeing it and mentioning it to the empress. She then pulled out her drawing pad and a piece of charcoal and sat by the small window to draw the map while it was still fresh in her mind.

Drawing was the one thing Jiayi knew she was good at. It helped her clear her mind and remember her visions. It was calming and enjoyable. She could easily draw for hours, lost in the simple act of dragging her bit of charcoal across the paper and bringing an image to life.

She was halfway done with the map when her mind started to drift and she remembered another image she had been working on the day before. She turned the page and admired the beautiful face of Prince Junjie. She ran her fingers around his jaw and lightly touched the strands of hair that fell over his forehead.

She shook her head and turned back to the map. She needed to focus. She had no idea when the empress might ask for the map, so she had to make sure it was completed as soon as possible.

But all she could think about was Prince Junjie. Where was he? What was he doing? Was he thinking of her? Was he safe?

She felt a sudden hitch in her throat. She knew that Prince Junjie's life ended in tragedy, but she didn't know any of the details. According to Zhihao, there were few records about Prince Junjie. He knew that the prince was famous for his good looks and that he had been betrayed and murdered when he was still a young man.

Jiayi stood and paced the room. It would only take a minute, she rationalized to herself. Once she knew that Junjie was safe, she could come back and finish her work on the map.

She pulled a thin cloth she used as a drape over her window and made sure the door was secure. When Eunuch Lo had been her minder, she had to keep her window uncovered and could not lock her door so he could check on her at any moment. Now that he was gone, Jiayi took some steps to ensure her own security by covering her window and make shifting a lock for her door.

Jiayi put on a pair of gloves and pried up a floorboard under her bed that hid the many items she had pilfered from the empress over the years. She pulled out the golden dragon and phoenix wedding necklace and climbed onto her bed, removing one of her gloves. She picked up the necklace and held it to her chest.

When she opened her eyes, she was standing behind Empress Wu in the audience hall of the palace in Chang'an. From the ache in her feet, she thought that the audiences must have already been going on for some time. She surveyed the room until her eyes landed on Prince Junjie. She smiled at him, and it took all her restraint not to give him a wave. She was in the body of Lady Meirong, one of the empress's ladies-in-waiting and nieces. While Junjie and Meirong were not yet married to anyone, they knew they would never be allowed to marry one another. Eventually, they would have to marry whoever the empress ordered them to. But until that day happened, they carried on their love affair in secret.

Junjie gave Jiayi a smile back and his eyes flitted to the exit. She gave him a nod so small it was nearly imperceptible. She then swooned, one of the other ladies catching her by the arm.

"Are you all right, Meirong?" the woman asked.

"Just a bit tired, I think," she said, putting her hand to her head. "I need to lie down, just for a moment."

"Shall I go with you?"

"No," Jiayi said a bit too quickly. "The empress will not

appreciate it if too many of us are absent. I am sure I can make it to my room safely."

The other woman helped her down from the dais, and then Jiayi slipped from the audience hall on her own. As she rounded a corner, Junjie was there waiting for her. He pulled her into his arms and pressed his lips to hers, caressing her face and neck. She drank him in, closing her eyes and losing herself in the sensations.

"How I missed you," she said.

"I only said goodbye a few hours ago when I slipped from your bed," he said with a naughty smile.

"So long ago," she whimpered, and he chuckled.

He took her hand and led her toward her room. She knew she shouldn't stay long. She should get back to drawing her map. But as Junjie ushered her into her room and closed the door behind him, she lost all sense of time and decorum and spent the afternoon wishing that her dreams were reality.

TWO

*W*hat if I can change the past?

Zhihao recalled Jiayi's words over and over again. He knew that she only meant changing what people knew about history. Correcting mistakes. Giving voice to people who had been lost or forgotten. Rediscovering stolen treasures. But he couldn't help but imagine what it would be like to actually change the past. The death of Eli, who had been his best friend back when he was a student in England, was a constant weight on his mind and heart. He knew, logically, that Eli's death had been a tragic accident. No one could have stopped it. And yet...yet he wondered...

"...and that was the first time I stepped onto the moon," Hu Xiaosheng said, crossing his arms and giving a satisfied nod.

Zhihao tried to make sense of the old man's words. "What?"

"I knew you were not paying attention!" Hu Xiaosheng said, wagging a bony finger at Zhihao.

"I was!" Zhihao said, dipping his writing brush in the ink even though it was already dripping with ink.

"Then what did I say?" Hu Xiaosheng asked. "Read back to me what you wrote."

Zhihao cleared his throat and looked down at the paper in front of him. "In 1825..."

Hu Xiaosheng waited expectantly, but that was all Zhihao had written before his mind wandered to Jiayi, as it did more and more these days.

"Ahh!" Hu Xiaosheng yelled. "I knew you were not paying attention. You are supposed to write down everything I say." Hu Xiaosheng was not just old, he was ancient. Hu Xiaosheng had no birth record to prove his age, but from the things he remembered as a child, Zhihao knew the old teacher was probably at least eighty years old. He'd been a young man during the early years of the Daoguang Emperor. One of Zhihao's primary duties was to write down whatever Hu Xiaosheng told him to. He was like a living history book, and it was essential to the university that his memories be collected before he died. Unfortunately for Zhihao, that often meant listening to the old man ramble on for hours without saying anything of importance.

"I know, I know," Zhihao said, putting down his writing brush and running his hands over his head. "I just...have a lot on my mind."

"You have one thing on your mind," Hu Xiaosheng said. "One woman." He nodded knowingly.

"She isn't the only thing on my mind," Zhihao insisted. "There's the empress, the seal, building a museum. But... yes, it is hard to concentrate on anything but Jiayi."

Hu Xiaosheng nodded and then rolled up some scrolls he had spread across the table. "Jiayi is precious," he finally said. "No one is like her. But she is timid. Easily frightened.

Like a white fox. Valuable, but if she ducks into her den, you will never coax her out."

Zhihao nodded. "I know. I care for her very much. If there was any way I could help her...get her away from the empress..."

"That would be very dangerous," Hu Xiaosheng said, raising an eyebrow as he made sure all his writing brushes were lined up in the correct order on their little rack.

"Of course," Zhihao said as he pushed his own papers aside and stretched. "I honestly don't see any way it would be possible. The empress would never willingly let Jiayi go. And there is nowhere I could take her. I can't leave my mother."

"Instead of focusing on what you cannot do," Hu Xiaosheng said, "think about what you can do for her."

"I almost feel as though I have done nothing for her," Zhihao said, "while she has done everything for me. I would never have found the emperor's seal without her."

"Sometimes, all we can do is wait," Hu Xiaosheng said. "The path will reveal itself in time."

Zhihao nodded and began pacing the room. He hoped the old teacher was right.

The door to the library opened and Jiayi stepped in carrying a long item wrapped in silk. Zhihao nearly tripped over his chair as he stepped forward to greet her. He heard Hu Xiaosheng chuckle behind him.

"Jiayi!" Zhihao exclaimed. "How pleasant to see you."

Jiayi's cheeks reddened, as they always did when anyone was kind to her. She looked down and gave a polite bend at the knees.

"Zhihao," she said. She held up the silk-wrapped package. "I have something for you."

As Zhihao accepted it, the silk slipped to the floor, revealing an incredible saber.

"It's beautiful," he said, angling the blade so he could see the etchings better in the light. "Who did it belong to? A general?"

"A queen," Jiayi said, picking up the silk from the floor and folding it. "The pirate queen Ching Shih."

"There was a pirate queen?" Zhihao asked.

Jiayi looked at him with surprise. "You haven't heard of Ching Shih?"

"To be fair," he said, "I haven't spent much time studying maritime history. But a female pirate sounds fascinating. I'm surprised I haven't heard of her."

"She wasn't just a pirate," Jiayi said. "There were lots of female pirates who served her. She was the leader of the pirates. She commanded five hundred ships! Thousands of men!"

Zhihao laughed. "Come now, surely if a woman were that powerful, I would have heard of her. You must be exaggerating."

Jiayi's face fell, and he knew that—not for the first time—he had hurt her feelings. But she cleared her throat and forced a smile to her lips. "Perhaps I was mistaken," she finally said. "But the sword is for you. The empress has no need of it anymore. She didn't even realize she left it with me. I thought it would make an interesting addition to the museum."

"It certainly will," he said. "Thank you. I will see what I can find out about her."

"I also need help with this," Jiayi said, pulling a folded piece of paper from her pocket and handing it to him.

Zhihao unfolded the paper and found a detailed map of

the East China Sea. "Did you draw this?" he asked. He knew that Jiayi was a talented artist.

"Yes," she said with a hint of pride. "From a map I saw when I was Ching Shih. She has a large amount of treasure buried here." She pointed to an island with a red circle drawn around it. "Once you figure out where this is, the empress wants us to meet with her."

"Well, if this pirate queen did exist," Zhihao said, "there could be important artifacts about her buried there."

"That would be very exciting, don't you think?" Jiayi asked, making a small clapping motion with her hands. "For the empress to send us on a ship to a faraway island to dig up buried treasure. I've never been on a ship before. Not in real life, anyway."

"It's horribly uncomfortable," Zhihao said offhandedly as he examined the map and tried to make sense of the archaic characters. He then realized how terribly rude he sounded and saw that he had once again dampened Jiayi's spirits. "But, yes, of course. It would be a wonderful adventure."

Jiayi nodded and went to greet Hu Xiaosheng. Zhihao chastised himself once more. He didn't know why he was so thoughtless with his words around her. He simply wasn't used to being in the company of someone who was little more than a slave. His own family was wealthy and he had been to school abroad. Until the day he met Jiayi, everyone in his life was rich, well-educated, and well-traveled. And yet, it was Jiayi who was the most fascinating person he had ever met. What he wouldn't give to help her escape her prison. See the world.

"Do you need help with that map?" Hu Xiaosheng called out.

Zhihao shook his head and returned to his work, forcing

himself to stop thinking about Jiayi for a moment, which was nearly impossible with her being in the same room.

"This…" he said, pointing to the top of the map, "is Jinzhou. You can tell by the size and way it juts out into the sea. Which would make these islands the Miaodao. I'm not familiar with the area, but a local person would be able to tell us exactly which island is circled when we get there."

"That's wonderful," Jiayi said. "You are so clever."

Zhihao brushed her off. "It was nothing. Your map is so detailed it was quite easy. You must have studied the map in your vision for some time."

She shook her head. "I barely had a glimpse of it."

"That's incredible," Zhihao said. "You have a fantastic memory. No wonder your English is coming along so well."

Jiayi blushed and fidgeted with her hair. Jiayi already knew a fair bit of English from the time she had spent in her visions in the bodies of European women. Zhihao was just helping her build her vocabulary and diction, and she had made remarkable progress in the few weeks they had been working together.

"If only I could read Chinese half as well," she finally said.

"You will," Zhihao said. "It is complicated for anyone to learn. But your handwriting, such as on the map, it quite well-formed."

"I'm just copying, though," she said. "I can't actually read and write on my own."

"Give it time," Hu Xiaosheng said. "You take on so much. Too much! Your brain needs to rest." Jiayi nodded and Hu Xiaosheng pulled out a sparkling purple crystal and handed it to her.

"What is this?" she asked but did not try to take it. She was wary of touching anything that might have a past.

"It is safe," he said. She still hesitated, but finally opened her hand to him. He dropped the stone into her palm. "It is called *zijing*. The next time you meditate, focus on this stone. It will help open your mind to all of the universe's possibilities."

She chuckled. "I think enough of the universe is already in my mind."

"But your powers have gotten stronger, haven't they?" Hu Xiaosheng asked, and Jiayi tentatively nodded.

"I have been able to stay in a vision much longer now than I could even a few weeks ago," she said. "And I am not so exhausted when I wake up."

Hu Xiaosheng had been helping Jiayi meditate and maintain more control over her visions. She had always thought that she was merely at the whim of the visions, tossed about in a storm. But in the months since she met Hu Xiaosheng and Zhihao, she had learned much more about her powers. Zhihao couldn't help but wonder just what she could do given time and training. She had already been able to exert some control over the hosts she traveled into. And she often retained their skills and abilities. He couldn't help but dream that it might just one day be possible for her to do so much more...

"Thank you," Jiayi said, clutching the *zijing* to her chest. She then turned to Zhihao. "We should go. The empress will be anxious to know where the treasure is buried."

"Of course," Zhihao said. "Go ahead to the palanquin. I just need to grab a few things."

She nodded and left as Zhihao went to grab his hat and coat.

"Third row, fourth shelf," Hu Xiaosheng said. "The scroll entitled 'The Widow Ching.'"

Zhihao went and found the scroll and brought it back to

Hu Xiaosheng. "What is it?" he asked as he threw his coat on, messing with the collar.

"An account of the Pirate Queen Ching Shih," Hu Xiaosheng said. Zhihao looked up and could feel the color drain from his face. "And it was one thousand ships. Not five hundred."

Zhihao cursed to himself and slapped on his hat as he rushed out the door. When was he going to learn to stop doubting Jiayi's visions?

"*S*o, while I cannot tell you the name of the exact island circled on Jiayi's map," Zhihao explained from his kneeling position on the floor in front of the empress, who was sitting high on a dais on her throne, "I am certain that it is among the Miaodao islands."

"Excellent!" the empress said. "Send for the admiral at once," she ordered one of her eunuch servants, who quickly left with a bow. "I knew you would not disappoint me, Zhihao Shaoye."

"I am sorry I could not be more specific," Zhihao said humbly. "But once Jiayi and I arrive in the region, I am sure the local people can point us in the right direction."

The empress scoffed. "You are not going to Miaodao."

"We aren't?" Zhihao asked. "But if this is the location of Ching Shih's treasure, there could be any number of arti-facts to discover. I should be there to catalog them."

"This isn't an archeological expedition," the empress said. "The money is for the empire. Do you know how much we lost in the rebellion?"

Zhihao bit his tongue. He knew all too well just how much land and money the empire lost after the foreigners stormed Peking and put an end to the Yihetuan Rebellion—and nearly overthrew the Qing Dynasty altogether. But for reasons he would never understand, the foreign powers allowed the empress to return to her place on the throne. Quite a missed opportunity, he thought. Not that he wanted China to become a vassal of foreigners, but it had been China's best chance to be rid of the Manchu once and for all. There might have been a Han emperor on the throne now. Or a president...

"But there is something else of great importance I must speak to you about," the empress continued. She waved her hand and Princess Der Ling, that odd looking woman with big eyes and snow-colored skin, stepped forward and opened a box before the empress. From the box, the empress lifted a large flat piece of jade carved into the shape of a phoenix.

"This ornament was once attached to the headdress that Empress Wu wore when she was first presented to Emperor Gaozong."

"You are certain?" Zhihao asked, glancing at Jiayi, who nodded.

"Yes," the empress said. "Jiayi confirmed it years ago. But since it was from before the woman became empress, I thought it of no value to me. But then I remembered where it came from. It was purchased by one of my ladies in a city market stall."

Zhihao nodded. It was not uncommon for people to sell items passed down in their families or discovered in their fields for a little extra cash. It was actually how many foreigners procured Chinese artifacts for museums abroad without ever getting their hands dirty.

"You know that Empress Wu's tomb was looted," the empress said.

"Hundreds of years ago," Zhihao said. "Probably not long after she was buried."

"I think the city markets could be full of items once owned by Empress Wu," the empress said. "I want for you and Jiayi to go into the city markets and find as many objects that came into contact with the empress as possible."

"Yes, Your Majesty," Zhihao said. Rifling through piles of junk in the hopes of finding a single item of value was not how Zhihao imagined being an archeologist, but he supposed there were worse ways to make a living.

"And there is someone else I wish for you to meet," the empress said. Through a side door, a young man entered. "This is Prince Kang, my nephew."

Zhihao and Jiayi bowed to the prince.

"He is going to work closely with you on this project," the empress said.

"Does he know anything about archeology?" Zhihao asked.

"No," the empress said. "But it is vitally important to him that you find an item that belonged to Empress Wu that can help me become an empress in my own right, just like she did. If I am declared empress, and not just empress-dowager, I will be able to appoint Kang as my heir."

Zhihao about choked as he tried to take a breath. Had the empress lost her mind? There already was an emperor. True, he was emperor in name only. After the empress returned to Peking, she'd had the emperor imprisoned in the Sea Palace within the Forbidden City. Occasionally, the empress would trot the man out for ceremonial events or show that he was still alive. But everyone knew that the empress was the real power in China. But still, for her to even consider appointing an heir of her own when the current emperor was still a young man was ridiculous. It was treason! Not that he cared if the empress was put to death. But why was she telling him this? He didn't want to be party to her machinations. What if the emperor found out? Zhihao—and his whole family—could be put to death for even listening to the empress speak in such a way. As he looked at Kang, the ladies-in-waiting, and the eunuchs, and then to Jiayi, he couldn't believe how unconcerned they all looked. Were they not worried about their very lives?

"I think he was struck speechless," Prince Kang said, and everyone, even the empress, chuckled.

"I am just surprised," Zhihao finally said. "The emperor—"

"Is of no concern," the empress interrupted. "You work for me. And now, you answer to Kang. Do I make myself clear?"

"Perfectly," Zhihao said through clenched teeth.

THREE

*J*iayi wondered why she had not seen Prince Kang before. While very few men were permitted within the women's quarters, family was the exception. She knew that as a servant, she was not supposed to look at a member of the royal family in the face unless instructed to do so. But she could not help but steal a glimpse of Prince Kang.

She blinked, lifting her eyes ever so slightly, and saw the prince smiling down at her. Even her guarded glance was caught by his dark smiling eyes. He had a wispy mustache and beard and wore a princely hat. She was surprised to see him wearing a yellow robe—all members of the royal family were technically permitted to wear yellow, but among male family members, it was a color usually reserved for the emperor—but at least the dragon embroidered on it only had four toes and not five. Only the emperor was ever allowed to wear a five-toed dragon.

Jiayi quickly looked away, but she felt her face blush and could feel that the prince was still looking at her.

"I look forward to working with you," the prince said,

his voice bright and friendly, as though he spoke with a smile. "With both of you."

Jiayi said nothing, but gave another bow of respect.

"You may speak to Kang about the details, Zhihao Shaoye," the empress said as she stood to leave.

"Yes, Your Majesty," Zhihao said, but Jiayi could tell he was not pleased.

Once the empress and her ladies had gone, Prince Kang approached Jiayi and Zhihao.

"I have heard much about the two of you," the prince said. Then he gave Zhihao the fist in palm salute. "I am honored."

Jiayi curtseyed, but Zhihao merely stood there with his arms crossed.

"So, how are you related to the empress?" he asked. "The empress's sister has no sons."

"True," he said. "I am the grandson of the empress's sister. My father is the magistrate of Shandong Province."

Jiayi could almost feel Zhihao groan. Prince Kang was low-ranking indeed. The son of a country magistrate? And the empress wanted to appoint him her heir? She couldn't imagine the ministers ever accepting him. And Jiayi didn't think the empress could ever appoint him as her heir anyway. As ineffectual as the emperor might be, she couldn't pretend that the man did not exist.

"I don't see how finding items that belonged to Empress Wu will help you or the empress get what you want," Zhihao said. "Perhaps if you explain your scheme more clearly, it will help with the search for...whatever we may find."

"The empress believes that by learning more about Empress Wu she will learn how she became an empress in her own right," Prince Kang explained. "If the empress can depose the emperor, she can appoint me as her heir."

Jiayi gasped and then covered her mouth. She looked around anxiously. Saying such words out loud was treason!

Kang looked at her and chuckled. "Don't worry. We are quite safe to talk here."

"This is foolishness," Zhihao grumbled. "No one item is going to give the empress the answer she seeks. Empress Wu's own son stepped down in her name. And she was very powerful. Women had more authority back then. The answers are in the historical records. But that was a thousand years ago. This is a different world. This empress will never be allowed to rule on her own."

"But the historical records are wrong," Jiayi said, looking up at Zhihao. "Isn't that one of the benefits of our work? Finding out the truth about the past. Rewriting history."

Zhihao sighed in frustration.

"The historical records once said that the emperor's seal was safely here in the Forbidden City, but we found it in the library," Jiayi continued. "History books might say that Empress Wu's son appointed her, but maybe there was more to it than that."

Jiayi was sure of it, in fact. She couldn't help but wonder if the dagger that Der Ling possessed was the answer. If that was the item that the empress needed. But she couldn't reveal her suspicions. She had promised to help Der Ling discover the secret of the dagger, and she did not want to disappoint her.

"Exactly," Prince Kang said, nodding his approval at Jiayi. She dared to look him full in the face, and he held her gaze. He did not turn away just because she was a lowly servant.

Jiayi nervously moved a strand of hair behind her ear.

She glanced at Zhihao, hoping to see approval there as well since he knew her words were true. But instead, she saw him glaring at Kang. She worried her lower lip. Working with both men was not going to be easy.

"So, we are just supposed to wander through the markets, randomly touching items, waiting for Jiayi to have a vision of Empress Wu?" Zhihao asked sarcastically.

Kang did not seem at all bothered by Zhihao's lack of confidence in the assignment. He chuckled. "You are the historian," he said. "The archeologist. I am sure you can come up with a better plan than that."

Zhihao's expression softened, and Jiayi had to silently appreciate Kang's ability to sooth Zhihao's ego.

"I suppose that the first step would be to find anything from that time period," Zhihao said. "While the markets are flooded with items from the last few hundred years, ever since the Manchu came to power, items from the Tang dynasty are much more rare. It would be easy for someone with a trained eye to spot real artifacts from the fakes."

"That sounds like an excellent place for your trained eye to start," Kang said. "Once you have found items you are sure date back to the right time period, Jiayi can then test them to see if any came into contact with Empress Wu."

"It would take time," Jiayi said. "I would have to recuperate between each session." Not to mention that the empress would undoubtedly have other work for her to do, more items for her to touch. And Der Ling would want her to touch the dagger. And she would like to have time to visit Prince Junjie. She had no idea how she was going to be able to keep up with the sudden demands on her powers. She would have to visit Hu Xiaosheng for help in strengthening her abilities.

"Excellent!" Prince Kang said, clapping his hands together. "I look forward to seeing what you will bring us."

With that, Jiayi knew that Zhihao was being dismissed, but he seemed reluctant to go. He glanced at Jiayi, and she thought maybe he was hoping she would ask him to stay, but it would not be proper and she couldn't think of anything she needed to speak to him about, so she only gave him a quick curtsey goodbye. Zhihao gave a stiff bow back to her and to Kang and then left the audience hall quickly.

"I don't think he likes me very much," Prince Kang said once Zhihao was out the door.

"He doesn't like anyone very much," Jiayi said, then she slapped her hand to her mouth. "Forgive me! That was unkind."

Prince Kang chuckled, and Jiayi realized she liked the sound of his laughter. It put her at ease, something she rarely felt around men. Even Zhihao.

"Will you walk with me, my lady?" the prince asked, motioning to the door of the audience hall.

"I will," Jiayi said. "But I'm no lady. If the empress has told you about me, you must know my lowly status."

"And if you know anything about me," the prince said, leading Jiayi to one of the many palace gardens, "you know that I was not born to be a prince, much less an emperor."

"But you are kin to the empress," Jiayi said. "Why have I not seen you before?"

"Before the empress got it into her head that I could be her heir, my family was an embarrassment to the empress," Kang said. "The empress's sister, my grandmother, is insane. My mother was disgraced as a young woman for falling in love with a farmer. She was sent to marry my father in Shandong as a punishment. My father was accused of corruption in his younger days and was unable to find a more suitable wife. It took them decades to rebuild their lives and reputations, though for some, the stains will never be washed clean."

"Those are serious charges," Jiayi said. "I am surprised that the empress would risk bringing you here. And to consider making you her heir...Will not the ministers be displeased?"

"It depends on who they dislike more," Kang said. "The empress or the emperor."

Jiayi pressed her lips in thought. If forced to choose, most people would support the empress over the emperor. In fact, most people already did. In reality, the empress should not wield as much authority as she did. The emperor should be running the country from his dragon throne—not imprisoned in the Sea Palace.

Jiayi finally shook her head. "It's all terribly complicated for me," she said. "I can only do as I am told."

The prince took a light hold of her elbow and turned her to him. "I think you can do much more than that," he said. Jiayi looked up at him, but when she saw the kindness in his eyes, she quickly looked away. "I heard you can speak many languages. Ride a horse. Even defend yourself from attack. You are smart and talented. Why are you even still here under my aunt's thumb?"

"Where else would I go?" Jiayi asked. "I have no friends or family outside these walls. I own nothing. I am not a servant, with the right to marry or earn a wage. The empress owns me, like one of her pet dogs."

Prince Kang narrowed his eyes at that. "That is not right," he said. "You are one of her ladies, answering her every call. You should be paid, and be able to plan a future for yourself."

Jiayi shrugged. "I would not dare anger her by asking for anything. If the empress dismissed me tomorrow, I would be destitute and alone. I shudder to think of what I would have to do to survive."

She knew what she would have to do. She'd done it before. As a child, she had been forced to steal items that could be sold so her family could eat. When she started having visions related to the items she touched, her mother sold her to a fortune teller. The woman claimed that Jiayi would be her apprentice. But in truth, she sold Jiayi almost immediately to the empress for ten times what she had paid Jiayi's mother. Jiayi had no desire to return to a life of stealing to survive.

"I will speak for you," Prince Kang said. "I will make sure your future is secure."

"No!" Jiayi exclaimed, gripping his robe. She then caught herself and let go, clearing her throat. "I mean, I can't have you risk angering the empress on my account. I am nothing. You could be emperor. Please, just leave things as they are."

"What kind of an emperor would I be if I allowed such an injustice to continue in my own home?" he asked. "Do not worry about me. I am in my aunt's favor. I should use that to my advantage while I can."

"But...why?" Jiayi asked. "Why would you do that for me? I'm nobody."

"You are not nobody," he said, reaching out and lightly tapping her nose. "You are the woman who is going to make me emperor." With that, he turned and walked away, still smiling.

Jiayi was struck speechless as she watched the prince walk away. He stopped for a moment to admire the beauty of one of the empress's prized chrysanthemum plants, and then continued on slowly, as though he didn't have a care in the world.

Jiayi reached up and rubbed her nose where he had touched her. He was certainly a kind man. And if he could do something for her, she would be most appreciative. But she didn't want him to risk his future for her. And she couldn't imagine him—or any man—offering to help her without wanting something in return. She would have to be on her guard. Prince Kang was easy to like, and perhaps too easy to trust.

"Watch out!" Der Ling snapped as Jiayi turned and walked right into her. Jiayi immediately kneeled down in front of the princess. She had been so lost in her thoughts, she hadn't even heard Der Ling approach.

"Forgive me," Jiayi said.

"I nearly tripped over you!" Der Ling said, reaching out and pulling Jiayi to her feet. "Are you all right?"

"Yes," Jiayi said. "Thank you."

"What did he want?" Der Ling asked, jutting her chin down the garden path that Prince Kang had taken. Jiayi stole a glance that way, but the prince was gone.

"He wanted to know more about my powers," Jiayi lied. She was suddenly struck with the awareness that the prince hadn't actually asked about her powers at all. Her powers were usually the only thing people wanted to talk to her about.

"What did you say?" Der Ling asked.

"Nothing he didn't already know," Jiayi said.

"That fool thinks he is going to be emperor someday," Der Ling sneered. "Can you believe such a thing?"

"I don't have an opinion," Jiayi said. "I only do as I am told."

Der Ling turned to Jiayi and laughed. "Why are you

lying to me?" she asked, pouting as though her feeling were hurt.

"I'm not, my lady!" Jiayi said with alarm. "I'd never—"

"If you only did as you were ordered," Der Ling said, "you would have told the empress about the dagger already. Why are you helping me if you don't have an opinion?"

"I...I..." Jiayi stammered. She had misspoken. She needed to be more careful with her words. She glanced around, looking for someone, anyone who might be able to serve as a distraction so she could get away.

"You hold great power in those little hands," Der Ling said, reaching out and taking Jiayi's hand, stroking her fingers. "Follow me." Der Ling quickly walked down one of the garden paths, tugging Jiayi behind her.

Jiayi blew out her cheeks and rushed to keep up with the princess, at least as quickly as she could in her pot-bottom shoes.

Der Ling took Jiayi to a secluded grotto and sat on a bench. She patted the seat beside her, as though inviting a dear friend for a private chat.

Jiayi sat on the edge of the bench in case she needed to bolt away at the slightest provocation.

"No one will see us here," Der Ling whispered conspiratorially, and she pulled the dagger out of her sleeve. It slightly unnerved Jiayi that Der Ling was walking around the Forbidden City with a weapon. If she were caught, she could be banished. "Touch it. Tell me what you see."

"You heard the empress's command," Jiayi said. "I need to conserve my energy for the work—"

"Touch it, dear Jiayi," Der Ling begged, but her voice had an edge to it and her smile quavered, as though she were on the verge of an eruption. "I have waited so long for more information."

Jiayi did as she was told, but when she woke up, she had nothing of note to tell Der Ling, which scared her more than if she had learned anything useful.

Der Ling was leaning forward, her smile revealing her teeth like a leering wolf. "So?" she asked. "What did you see?"

Jiayi racked her mind, trying to come up with something that would satisfy Der Ling's desire. She had been Empress Wu, but she had only been hosting an audience, listening to petitioners complain about the harvest and other matters. She had felt the dagger strapped to her thigh, but she never touched it. Nothing of importance had happened that she knew of.

"The dagger..." Jiayi started, "is—*was* very important to her. She carried it with her all the time."

Der Ling nodded. "And?"

Jiayi's mind was frozen. She had no idea what to do or say. She was terrified and couldn't think. She slipped from the bench and kneeled before the princess.

"Nothing," she cried, tears falling down her face. "I saw nothing! I'm sorry I failed you."

Der Ling sighed and sat back on the bench. She replaced the dagger in her sleeve and bit her lower sip as she thought. She then leaned forward and Jiayi flinched, certain Der Ling was going to strike her, but the blow never came.

"Then we will just have to try again," Der Ling said. "Right?"

"Yes, Your Highness," Jiayi said quickly.

"As soon as you are ready, come see me in my quarters." Der Ling stood and walked out of the grotto, but then she turned back. "I expect to see you again soon, Jiayi."

Jiayi bent forward, placing her forehead to the ground. "Yes, Your Highness!"

Jiayi waited until she could no longer hear Der Ling's footsteps before she dared raise her head from the dusty path.

It was a long walk back to Jiayi's room, so she sat in the grotto for a while, waiting for her heart to stop thumping before she moved. She didn't want anyone to see her in such a disheveled state. She wasn't exactly sure why she was so upset, other than she felt completely overwhelmed and out of her depth. Everyone wanted something from her, and she didn't know how to live up to their expectations.

She ran her hands over her gown, trying to smooth it as much as possible and wipe the dirt away. As she did so, she felt the gemstone that Hu Xiaosheng had given her roll about in one of her sleeve pockets. She pulled the gemstone out and cupped it in her palm like a precious egg. She then held it to her chest and closed her eyes, taking a few deep breaths. She felt her heart rate slow and her mind calm.

After a moment, she began to think about Prince Junjie. She could see his face so clearly. She could then see his neck, his chest, his arms. Then, it was as if the man was standing right in front of her. He gave her a smile and opened his mouth to speak.

"Hello," he said.

She gave him a polite nod.

"What is your name?" he asked.

Jiayi was surprised. Was she having a vision from before he met Lady Meirong? Or was this not a vision at all, just her imagination.

"I am Lady Meirong," she said. "Do you not know me?"

The prince chuckled. "You are not Meirong. But I have seen you before. What is your real name?"

"Jiayi," she said.

"Jiayi," he repeated. "Beautiful. Do you use the characters for auspicious and joyous?"

Jiayi had no idea, but she nodded anyway. She liked his description.

He then stepped closer, holding out his hand. She reached out to take it, but just when they touched, the vision faded away. She opened her eyes and was sitting in the grotto.

She sighed in disappointment. It was only a dream.

FOUR

"*Y*ou see something you like?" a dark-skinned elderly man asked Zhihao as he wandered through one of Peking's many city markets.

"Not particularly," Zhihao lied. He had made his way to this stall after another vendor told him the man was known for his Tang Dynasty era goods. Most of what the man had on display was not that old. Dozens of bronze statues of frogs, lions, and horses were crowded on one table, along with some wooden door carvings and a few knives. Mostly items that could be found in any home. But he could see a ceramic statue of a woman on the back of a horse peeking out from under a cloth. Those were very popular during the Tang Dynasty, a time when women were allowed to play polo along with men.

The man chuckled and rubbed his fingers together. Had he seen through Zhihao's ruse?

"A man of discerning taste," the vendor said. "I know what you like."

From under the table, the man pulled out a square item wrapped in silk. He motioned for Zhihao to step into the tent, away from the eyes of passersby. The man flipped the silk back and revealed a high-quality carving in soapstone of a graphic erotic scene. A nude man and woman were reclined on a large bed, the woman's body poised to accept her lover, and the man eager to attend her. The carving was exceptionally detailed.

Zhihao scoffed and stepped out of the tent. The item was not rare or old. Such pornographic displays had grown in popularity over the years and were easily purchased if a person knew where to look.

The man laughed as he placed the carving back in its hiding place. "Come, come, sir!" the man said, following him. "What are you looking for? I am sure I can find whatever you desire."

"Tang era items," Zhihao finally admitted. "The real thing. I'll know if you try to sell me a fake."

The man scratched his chin. "Tang, hmm? Quite rare. Very difficult to procure."

Unfortunately, the man wasn't lying. Zhihao knew how precarious old terracotta and porcelain were. Finding a piece that was whole was nearly impossible. Most people who discovered them were farmers, and they didn't take care to make sure the items were removed from their fields in one piece.

"Are you saying that statue there is fake?" Zhihao asked, pointing to the polo-playing woman under the cloth.

The man clicked his tongue in annoyance when he realized the statue was not adequately covered. "*Aiya*!" He pulled up the cloth to go ahead and show Zhihao the piece.

Zhihao covered his mouth with his hand to make it look as if he was considering the item, but in truth, he was trying to make sure he did not show just how pleased he was with what he was looking at. The statue was in perfect condition.

The woman's head was slightly cocked to the side as she gripped a polo stick in one hand and nothing in the other. Originally, the horse's reins and bridle would have been made of leather, which had long since dissolved. But the woman's top knot, her hands, and all four of the horse's legs were intact. Not a chip or crack to be seen.

"This only just arrived," the man said. "I haven't had time to evaluate it properly."

Zhihao chuckled to himself. The only "evaluation" these sellers did was compare notes to see how much they might be able to get for them from the right person.

"How much?" Zhihao asked.

The man looked Zhihao up and down, most likely considering what a man like Zhihao could afford more than what the statue might actually be worth. The man then gave a number that made Zhihao bark with laughter. He didn't even try to hide his expression.

"Are you serious?" Zhihao asked. He knew that even the empress would not pay that much unless she knew it was exactly what she was looking for. Maybe he would have to bring Jiayi down here after all and have her test the items before he considered buying anything.

"That is a good price, sir," the merchant said, using the cloth to wipe some dust from the woman's face. "Because you are local. Do you know what those stupid foreigners will pay for a piece like this?"

Zhihao grimaced at that. He well knew that British and American merchants could easily spend a thousand pounds on trinkets in a Chinese market and then sell them back home for ten or twenty times the price, or more for just the right item for just the right buyer. The British especially loved to decorate their homes with exotic far-eastern treasures.

Zhihao was debating what to do. This was a Tang Dynasty item, but he had no idea if the empress would reimburse him for the cost. Was it likely that Empress Wu had come into contact with such an item anyway? He sighed over the ridiculousness of the task. It was like trying to dredge a needle from the bottom of the ocean.

"There you are!"

Zhihao nearly jumped as his friend Lian suddenly gripped his shoulders and shouted a greeting in his ear.

"What are you doing in this dreadful place?" Lian asked as Zhihao straightened his cuffs.

"Getting ripped off, I think," Zhihao said, looking back to the vendor.

The man put his hand to his heart. "You wound me, sir. I'm just as honest and hardworking as you."

"Is that why you are trying to pass off that cheap Tang imitation as real?" Lian asked, pointing to the statue.

"This is certainly a Tang terracotta sculpture," the merchant said, his voice rising in annoyance.

"Did your wife make it?" Lian asked, riling the man up. Zhihao was certain the sculpture was real, but Lian was probably better at haggling than he was.

"You don't want it?" the man asked, tossing the cloth back over the statue. "Then you leave! I won't do business with men like you."

Lian just laughed and tugged Zhihao away from the stall. Zhihao nearly dug his heels into the ground to keep from being dragged along. He was still undecided on the sculpture. But then his eyes fell on something else.

"Wait!" he said, pulling his arm from Lian's grip. On the table, among the shiny bronze statues, was a small green disk. Zhihao picked it up and turned it over in his hand. It was ornately carved with phoenix feathers on one side, but was smooth on the other.

"How much for this?" he asked the vendor.

The man hemmed and hawed for a moment before giving a surprisingly small number. Zhihao pulled the coins out of his pocket and handed them over without bothering to haggle. He then walked off with Lian.

"What is it?" Lian asked, taking the disk from Zhihao.

"A Tang era mirror," Zhihao said. "It's actually bronze but hasn't been shined in a while. The smooth side should be clear enough to see your reflection in."

"It's in terrible shape," Lian said, but as far as Zhihao knew, the condition of the item didn't matter to Jiayi's visions. And if the mirror wasn't useful to the empress, it might make a nice gift for Jiayi to keep.

"My mother can clean it up," Zhihao said, slipping the mirror into his pocket. "So, why were you looking for me?"

"I can't stop thinking about that court historian you work with," Lian said, and Zhihao looked away. "I would really love to meet her."

"Why?" Zhihao asked.

"Because you know my area of expertise is government," Lian said. "If I could talk to someone inside the palace about the history of China's ruling class, I am sure I could glean all sorts of knowledge from her."

Zhihao cleared his throat as he tried to find a way out of this. It was common knowledge that Zhihao was working for the empress to reclaim China's lost history. It was less commonly known that Jiayi was the real reason Zhihao had discovered anything of note. After all, Zhihao could hardly announce to the world that he was working with a woman who could see through time. People would think he was crazy. And if they thought he was telling the truth, it could put Jiayi in danger. She suffered enough abuse at the hand of the empress. What would happen to her if everyone wanted to test her powers? It was in Jiayi's best interest to keep her abilities a secret.

But after Zhihao and Jiayi discovered the emperor's seal, Zhihao had been desperate to find a way to save Jiayi from the empress. He had confided in Lian that he had been working with a girl at the empress's court. To hide her abilities, he only said that she was a "court historian." But he supposed he should have known better than to call her that to another historian. If she had access to otherwise secured historical documents, of course people like Lian would want to speak with her.

"You know men are not allowed to access the inner court of the women," Zhihao said. "I can't just take you there."

"I know that," Lian said. "But I have heard that a young lady has been visiting you and Hu Xiaosheng at the library. It's her, isn't it?"

Zhihao cursed to himself. "Yes, it's her."

"Fantastic!" Lian said. "When is she coming again? I'll be there to meet her."

"I'm not sure," Zhihao said, and for once he wasn't lying. "She has to answer to the empress at any given moment. She never knows when she might have the time to slip away and talk to Hu Xiaosheng or me."

"The next time she comes, then," Lian persisted, "send for me. I'm usually in my office if I'm not in class."

"Sure," Zhihao said, unable to think of any other way to get out of agreeing for the moment. He supposed he would have to tell Jiayi to stop coming to the library for a while. Though, he knew that would make her terribly sad—and him too. Sometimes the only thing that helped him get through the monotony of the day was the slight chance that Jiayi could show up at any moment. He felt the weight of the mirror in his pocket and smiled to himself as he imagined the look on her face when he handed it to her. She was so easy to please.

"Is there something going on between you and that girl?" Lian suddenly asked.

"What?" Zhihao scoffed. "No. Why?"

"Because you have a stupid dreamy look on your face."

Zhihao reached up and wiped his face as though Lian had said there was a spot of sauce on it. "I...I don't know what you mean."

"Mmhmm," Lian said with a smirk. "What's the girl's name?"

"Jiayi," Zhihao said, and Lian burst into laughter. "What?"

"That!" Lian said. "You can't say her name without smiling. You are smitten with the girl."

Zhihao rolled his eyes and sighed. "Don't be ridiculous."

"No, I'm happy for you. You've hardly looked twice at any woman since coming back. Not since..." Lian caught himself before he said her name and the humor in the atmosphere died.

"Not since Rebecca," Zhihao finally finished for Lian, and Lian gave a small nod.

Zhihao had foolishly fallen in love with a British classmate while he was in school. He was certain he would have married her—much to the disappointment of his mother—if only Rebecca's brother Eli had not tragically died while the three of them were excavating a pyramid in Egypt. The loss of Eli had wounded both Zhihao and Rebecca deeply, creating a wedge between them. Eventually, Zhihao returned home, and Rebecca stayed in England. He had promised her that he would write to her every week, but he never did.

"There's no shame in it if you do like this girl," Lian said. "I'm sure your mother is tired of waiting for grandchildren."

Zhihao's mother had already given him her tacit approval to marry Jiayi if he wanted to. But it wasn't possible. Jiayi was not free to marry. She was the property of the empress, and the empress valued her for her abilities. She would never let Jiayi go.

"It's not that simple," Zhihao mumbled.

"Life rarely is," Lian said. "But once I meet her, I'll be sure to let you know if she meets with my approval or not."

"If I know you," Zhihao said, "you would disapprove of her most fervently, making sure I cut off all contact with her just so you can swoop in and marry her for yourself."

"That fetching, is she?" Lian asked. "Well, if you don't claim her hand soon, maybe I'll consider doing just that. Who wants a wife that only totters around the house making babies and embroidering endless piles of tiny shoes anyway?"

"I don't think wives make babies on their own," Zhihao said.

"A partner," Lian went on. "That's what a man truly needs. A woman who can support a man in his endeavors. Have stimulating conversations. The education of women is vitally important. How did Jiayi come to be such an expert on history? Her father must have been an enlightened man."

"I'm not exactly sure," Zhihao said. "She doesn't like to talk about herself much."

"Beautiful, smart, and humble?" Lian said. "You are selling me more and more on this woman by the moment."

Zhihao groaned to himself. He was getting tired of

thinking of Lian courting Jiayi. He then remembered the way Prince Kang and Jiayi were looking at each other during the audience with the empress and felt even more annoyance.

"What do you know about Prince Kang?" Zhihao asked Lian in an attempt to divert the conversation.

"Prince Kang?" Lian asked, his steps slowing. "What do you mean?"

Zhihao had to wait for Lian to catch up with him. "The empress's nephew. Do you know of him?"

"I...have heard his name," Lian said. "Why?"

"I met him when I had an audience with the empress," Zhihao said. He was forbidden from speaking about his conversations with the empress, but he didn't think there was any rule about speaking of other people he met within the walls of the Forbidden City.

Lian stopped suddenly, grabbing Zhihao by the shoulder. "You met him at court?" Lian asked.

"Yes," Zhihao said. "Why? Is that important?"

"It might be," Lian said. "He's...known to me, and to some of my associates."

Zhihao knew that Lian was talking about his revolutionary friends. People who followed the teachings of Dr. Sun.

"But Kang is a prince," Zhihao said. "How can he have such...leanings?"

"We thought he did," Lian said. "But now I wonder."

Zhihao leaned in and spoke in barely more than a whisper. "Do you think he would betray you?"

Lian's ordinarily placid face furrowed in worry. "I must go," Lian said.

"Is there anything I can do?" Zhihao called after him.

"Just find out whatever you can and let me know everything!" Lian called back as he rushed out of the market.

Zhihao sighed, wondering if he shouldn't have said anything about Kang. Zhihao was no supporter of the Manchu and the empress, but he wouldn't quite say he was revolutionary either. His family had greatly benefitted from their association with the empress, and he appreciated some of the strides she had made toward reforming the government. But it had not been enough. And he would not be sad the day Manchu rule came to an end. But if Kang had democratic ideas and the empress wanted him to be the next emperor, he could be the man to change China for the better. He could usher in a more constitutional style monarchy. Perhaps establish a parliament.

Or he could have just been pretending he was a revolutionary to learn who the most dangerous traitors to the throne were. Lian's friends could be under arrest right now. Even Lian himself could be in danger.

So could Zhihao. If the empress knew that Zhihao associated with a revolutionary, he could be counted among their number. He and his whole family could be arrested and executed without even a trial.

Zhihao rushed back to the library. He needed to get a message to Jiayi. Kang could be a danger to all of them.

FIVE

*J*iayi slipped out of the palace early in the morning, when she was sure that Zhihao would be teaching a class. He clearly did not like Kang. And since Kang was living in the palace and had been kind to her, she was sure that Zhihao would have lots of questions about him for her that she would not want to answer.

She wore a simple gown and plaited her hair, topping her head with a woven hat to shield her face from the sun and appreciative glances. Everywhere she went, she felt men's eyes on her, no matter how plainly she dressed or quickly she walked. In fact, before she was even allowed to exit the western gate of the Forbidden City, she had to be searched by two of the palace guards to make sure she was not stealing anything. One of the guards in particular liked to linger as he ran his long fingers over her breasts and rear end. Just a glance from him made her sick, much less feeling his hands on her body. After she was free from his grasp, she nearly ran to the nearest market street and away from his protracted gaze.

Once she was out of sight of the palace, she bought two pork buns and nibbled on them while her stomach settled and she looked at the precious silks, jars of wine, carved bamboo fans, and other items that were for sale. She felt the coolness of a jade pendant in her shoe, one stolen from the empress, and her heart raced.

Over the years, she had pilfered many items that the empress had given her to touch and then forgot about. She had always considered them to be her insurance for the day when the empress finally tired of her so she would not be completely penniless. But what good were beautiful combs and shining jewels? She needed money. So today, she brought one of the necklaces with her, a small jade carving of a butterfly on a chrysanthemum, in the hopes of selling it. She had no idea what it could be worth. She had very little experience with using money since she had been sold to the palace. But any cash would be more than she had now. She wandered past a stall selling jade, both raw pieces and stones carved and polished into beautiful necklaces and bracelets.

"What can I do for you, pretty girl?" the seller asked, turning to face her. He looked her up and down and licked his lips.

Jiayi took another nervous bite of her *baozi* and said nothing. She reached into her shoe and ran her fingers over the smooth jade of the pendant.

"You looking for something to buy?" the man asked. "A bit of good luck for your baby? Or did your mistress send you to buy a new bauble for her hair?"

"I...I want to...sell..." she said so softly she could barely hear her own voice.

"What? Speak up!" the man said, leaning into her and cupping his ear.

Jiayi gulped, nearly choking on her steamed bun, and then turned away. But before she took a step, she felt a rough hand grip her wrist. She dropped the last of her bun and turned to slap the man, but it wasn't the man who had grabbed her. It was an older woman.

The woman waved the man—probably her son—away and beckoned Jiayi closer to her with a crook of her finger.

"You have something to sell?" the old woman asked. "Maybe your young mistress sent you to part with one of her father's gifts."

Jiayi relaxed a little. The woman was telling her what to say. She had probably bought many items maids stole from their mistresses.

"Yes," Jiayi said with a nod. "My mistress sent me. She... she needs money."

The woman moved into a shaded area of the stall and motioned for Jiayi to follow. "Show me."

Jiayi looked around, but no one seemed to be paying them any mind. She pulled out the pendant. The woman reached out to touch it, but Jiayi snapped her hand shut. The woman pressed her thin lips in annoyance.

"How much?" Jiayi asked.

"Such a small piece," the woman said as she opened a purse and pulled out three coins. "Not worth much."

Jiayi snorted. "More." She didn't know how much it was worth, but she was certain the woman would try to pay as little as possible for it. As a child, Jiayi would sell the items she stole so she could buy food for her mother and sisters. She hadn't known much about the value of things back then either, but she at least knew that if she waited, the merchants always offered more.

The woman tisked and then pulled out not one, but two more coins. "This is all I can offer," she said.

Jiayi shook her head and then made a simpering face. "If I go back with too little, my mistress will beat me."

"*Aiyo!*" the woman said, finally offering Jiayi ten coins. "No more!"

Jiayi smiled and opened her hand. The woman swiped the jade pendant away quickly, depositing the coins in its place. Jiayi slipped the coins into her pocket and started to leave, but then she stopped.

"Jewels," Jiayi said.

The woman shook her head. "I don't buy jewels."

"Where can I sell them?" Jiayi asked. "A safe place."

The woman hesitated, but then spoke to Jiayi in a low voice. "You must be careful, young miss. If you sell too much too quickly, people will notice."

Jiayi nodded. "I understand."

"Not here," the woman continued. "Don't sell too much in the same place. Harbin Road for jewels. Yonghe Temple for silks. Blooming Spring Lane for gold. But you can bring me more jade."

"I will," Jiayi said. "Thank you."

As Jiayi left the stall, her heart was fluttering in her chest. She did it! She sold something. And she made a good contact to sell more. She had a few more jade pieces, but mostly what she had were gold and jewels. She knew that the jade piece was worth more than what she had gotten for it, but jade was worthless to her. She was now ten coins richer than she had been in years.

She continued to walk and held her face up to the sun. Maybe she was no longer as trapped as she once was. After all, only a year ago, the empress would never have let Jiayi leave the palace, especially on her own. But since she started working with Zhihao, the empress allowed her to travel to and from the library unescorted. After Eunuch Lo died, the empress said she was going to find Jiayi a new escort, but she never did.

As Jiayi reached the end of the market street, she knew that the port was to the south. If she had enough money, she could flee right now. Board a ship and sail to a new world. A new life. Of course, it would be dangerous. Even walking in Peking could be perilous for a woman alone. And Zhihao had said something about many ports being closed to Chinese women. She didn't know anything about that. It would be terrible to sail all the way to a new country just to be sent back to China. She also couldn't read more than a few characters. If anyone wanted her to sign a contract, she wouldn't be able to read it. She knew that many women often ended up as slaves in brothels or sold to cruel husbands. She thought about how she almost stupidly got onto a ship with Marcus and the man in the white suit before she saw the women in bondage below deck.

No, she couldn't just leave. She needed a plan. She needed help. But she had no idea where to get it. No one in the palace would help her escape. And Zhihao had so far been useless in coming up with a plan.

She grunted to herself in frustration as she turned in the direction of the library. But she wouldn't lose heart. She still had many more items to sell before she could even think about leaving. One step at a time, she would figure out a plan.

*W*hen Jiayi reached the library, she was surprised that Hu Xiaosheng wasn't in his usual spot, hunched over an ancient text mumbling to himself. While she waited, she wandered down some of the rows of shelves that were packed full of scrolls and artifacts.

She ignored most of the scrolls since she couldn't read them. She had looked at some before and realized that even if she could read, she wouldn't be able to make any sense of the old style of writing many of the scrolls used. Hundreds of years ago, Chinese characters were completely different from how they were now.

As she walked, her eyes fell on a pretty cloisonné box that wasn't Chinese in style. In fact, it looked like a jewelry box she once saw when she was in the body of a French woman. She let her sleeves fall over her hands and she took the box down from the shelf. She giggled when she looked at the lid and saw an image of three women lounging on a couch and chairs. They wore huge puffy dresses, their skin was white as milk, and their hair was piled on top of their heads like clouds. When she opened the box, she quickly slammed it shut again when she heard a tinkling noise.

She looked around and listened, but when she was satisfied that no one heard her, she opened it again. The tinkling resumed, and she realized the box was playing a song. She thought the simple melody was utterly charming. After a moment, the song stopped. She shook it, but nothing happened. She turned it over and found a small key. She turned it, and the music repeated the same pleasant tune. She thought it was an absolutely lovely device and let the song run until the key wound down.

Jiayi looked around to make sure no one had found her when she was distracted. Then, she pulled the coins out of her pocket and put them into the box. She crouched down and placed the box behind a stack of dusty scrolls that hadn't been touched in ages. She realized that it would be better if she hid her money outside of the palace instead of back in her room. Even though she couldn't keep an eye on it here, if the empress ever tossed her out suddenly, she would not be able to go back to her room to collect her money or jewels. By hiding the money here, she would always have access to it. She stood up and nodded to herself, pleased that the box was well hidden. This would be the next step in her plan. She would sell her stolen items and then hide the cash here.

"Jiayi?"

She turned and saw Hu Xiaosheng at the end of the row, leaning on his cane. She gave a bow and then rushed to him.

"Hu Xiaosheng," she said. "I was just exploring while waiting for you."

"I hope you were not waiting long," he said as he slowly lumbered to his usual chair at a long table where several scrolls were laid out, along with a stack of papers, a writing brush, and an inkstone and ink stick. As Hu Xiaosheng sat down, he reached for a cool teapot, pouring the water onto the inkstone. He then picked up the ink stick and ran it over the wet stone, turning the solid stick into liquid ink for writing.

Jiayi sat across from him and watched the smooth repetitive motion of the stick moving over the stone. It was almost hypnotizing.

"No," Jiayi said. "I arrived later than I planned. I suppose Zhihao will be here soon."

"He comes and goes as he wishes," Hu Xiaosheng said. He finished preparing his ink, placed the ink stick aside, and picked up his writing brush. He dipped the brush into the ink several times, dabbing it on the side of the stone until he had just the right amount of ink on the brush, then he began writing on a blank piece of paper. His strokes were quick and clean, and in only a moment, he already had several characters written. Jiayi was fascinated that the characters made any sense to him at all.

"Hu Xiaosheng," she said after watching him for several minutes, "could you teach me to write my name?"

He stopped mid-character and offered her the brush. He slid a blank piece of paper to her, along with the ink stone. He then moved around the table to stand beside her.

"Writing is not simply drawing lines on a page," Hu Xiaosheng said. "It is the physical expression of the beauty within one's heart and mind. Only if your spirit is balanced will you be able to write what your heart truly wants to communicate."

"I just want to write my name," Jiayi said.

"Why?" Hu Xiaosheng asked.

Jiayi blushed as she thought about her vision of Prince Junjie in the garden the day before. She had been so flattered when he said her name was beautiful, she was struck with guilt for feeling proud of his attention, even if it had only been in her mind.

Jiayi dropped the brush. "I'm sorry," she said. "I shouldn't have asked. I'm too stupid to be able to understand such things."

Hu Xiaosheng picked up the brush and placed it back in her hand. "All strokes must be placed in the correct order for the character to look correct," he explained, ignoring the way she disparaged herself. "Top before bottom, left before right. Understand?" She nodded. "I don't suppose you know which characters make your name? Different characters can have the same pronunciation."

"I am not sure," she said. "But I think they are 'auspicious' and 'joyous.'"

Hu Xiaosheng considered this for a moment as he stroked his long white beard. "Who gave you this name?"

Jiayi opened her mouth to say her mother, but then she remembered that her mother had given her the milk name Sparrow. She tried to remember the first time someone called her Jiayi and she recalled the day her mother sold her to a fortune teller, a woman named Madam Liu.

"A stranger," Jiayi said. "A fortune teller. She gave me this name after she bought me. She said I needed a better name if she was going to present me to the empress."

The old man nodded. "I do not think a woman like that would use 'joyous' if she wanted to impress the empress with your powers." He then took the brush and leaned over the paper. Starting in the top left corner, he began to paint the strokes of Jiayi's name.

"Auspicious, yes," he said. "But for the second character, I think 'to remember' is more appropriate."

Twelve strokes were needed to make the "jia" character, and then fourteen for "yi." Jiayi shook her head in astonishment. She did not think she would be able to remember all those strokes to write her name, much less ever learn to read a book's worth of characters.

"That is so complicated," Jiayi lamented as Hu Xiaosheng gave her the brush. She leaned over the paper, but Hu Xiaosheng stopped her, leading her hand to the inkstone so she would have enough ink to write with.

"Clear your mind of everything else," Hu Xiaosheng said. "This is a private conversation between you and the ink and the paper. Listen to what your heart wishes to say."

Jiayi exhaled and used her left hand to hold back her right sleeve so it would not smear the ink. She held the brush tight like a chopstick.

"Gently," Hu Xiaosheng said, tapping her hand until her

wrist flopped like a wet noodle, "and keep your elbow and arm straight. Use your fingers to direct the movements. Feel the energy flow from your heart, through your arm and fingers into the brush."

Jiayi nodded and finally let the brush touch the paper. She looked at the example Hu Xiaosheng had done for her and tried to follow the same order, but she knew she got some of them wrong. But as she worked, Hu Xiaosheng said nothing, so she was not sure if she was writing correctly or not. When she was done, she stood upright and chuckled to herself.

It looked terrible. The lines were fat and crooked, making it look more like a blob than an elegant representation of her name. But Hu Xiaosheng nodded and his eyes shone.

"Your heart is full of innocence and wonder," he said, "but there is deep knowledge there as well."

"You can see that in my writing?" she asked.

"No," he said. "Your writing is hideous. But I know you are eager to learn."

They both laughed and Jiayi felt much more at ease about her lack of writing skill.

"I will give you a writing kit to take back to your room," Hu Xiaosheng said. "You will improve with practice."

"Thank you," Jiayi said.

They heard the door open and Zhihao walked in carrying a stack of books.

"Jiayi!" he said when he saw her. "I wasn't expecting you."

"I slipped out early so the empress wouldn't miss me," she said.

He nodded. "Let me take care of a few things, and then

we can talk. I thought we could go to a marketplace together."

"I look forward to it," she said and hoped the nervousness did not show in her voice. She had wanted to avoid Zhihao, and now she would be spending several hours with him. She only hoped they would be visiting a market other than the one she had already been to that morning.

SIX

*T*here was something different about Jiayi today, Zhihao thought as they rode together in a hired rickshaw to the Yonghe Temple market street. She seemed...happy.

"What were you and Hu Xiaosheng working on together?" he asked.

She smiled but shyly tucked a strand of hair behind her ear. "He was teaching me how to write my name," she said as she pulled a rolled up piece of paper out of a bag that Hu Xiaosheng had given her as they left the library. As she unfurled the paper, he couldn't help but let out a surprised laugh.

"I thought you were a skilled artist?" he said as he looked at her terrible attempt.

"I am not," she said. "I just...sketch things. And this isn't art, it's writing."

"Writing is a form of art," he insisted. "You still use a brush and ink. With a little practice, I'm sure your writing will improve immensely."

"Thank you," she said. "That's what Hu Xiaosheng said.

He gave me a writing kit to practice with. I think reading would be a more useful skill than writing, though."

"We should work on that," Zhihao said, remembering it was one of the things he had promised to teach her. He had been so busy since they found the emperor's seal, he hadn't found the time. But then he remembered Lian wanting to meet her and bristled at the idea of her being at the library so often. Perhaps they should find another location to meet and discuss the empress's assignment.

Zhihao cleared his throat and rubbed his hands together. "I was thinking that maybe we should not meet at the library quite so often. Perhaps I should come to the Forbidden City instead."

"What?" she asked, her eyes going big in surprising alarm. "Why?"

"I...uh..." He hadn't quite expected her to be so against the idea. "Well, with us hopefully collecting more items, it might be easier for you to stay closer to home. I would hate to make you even more exhausted by forcing you to travel to the library."

"You aren't forcing me," she said. "I enjoy it. And Hu Xiaosheng is so old. It would be difficult for him to come to me."

Zhihao tried to force a smile. "Of course," he said and then turned away, watching as the rickshaw traveled down the crowded street. He rubbed his chin as he tried to come up with another idea. It was usually a source of gossip around campus whenever Jiayi paid a visit. Few women were ever seen at the university, and everywhere Jiayi went, heads turned. Lian was certain to hear about Jiayi's morning visit. He would already want to know why Zhihao didn't send for him. He wouldn't be able to make excuses for not introducing them forever.

They arrived at Yonghe Temple Street, which was lined with vendors along either side that formed a ramshackle marketplace. Zhihao reached up and helped Jiayi down from the rickshaw, holding onto her hand a little longer than necessary, but he noticed that she did not pull away until he finally let go.

"So, why did you want to come here?" he asked her as they entered the market.

"I've never been here," she said. "I don't travel so far from the palace on my own. There is another market near the palace that I explore when I visit the library sometimes."

Zhihao nodded. "I'm not sure we will find much here. Since the temple is nearby, most items here will be for the dead."

Jiayi nodded as she passed stalls of incense, paper money, and stone ancestor tablets waiting to be inscribed. Her hands were tucked deep into her long sleeves to keep from touching anything.

At one table, among mostly earthenware pots, Zhihao spied a silver bowl, cup, and pitcher that seemed to be in a Tang-era style. They appeared to be in quite good condition, however, so he was not sure if they were from the Tang era or simply in the same style but manufactured later.

"What are you looking at?" Jiayi asked him.

He nodded toward the silver items. "Those look promising, but I can't be sure that they are actually old or just made to look old."

Jiayi shook her head. "I wouldn't have any idea."

The stall's merchant, a young man, came forward and picked up a stack of bowls. "All handmade by my family, sir," he said. "Excellent quality! How many do you want?"

"Did you make those silver pieces?" Zhihao asked.

"No, sir," the man said. "We bury the pots in the ground to irrigate our farmland. I dug those up myself."

Zhihao and the man haggled back and forth a bit, and just as they were about to come to an agreement on a price, Zhihao heard Jiayi call his name. She sounded frantic. He looked down the row but did not see her amongst the crowd.

"Jiayi?" he called.

"Hurry!" she yelled back.

He pushed past a few people who shot him annoyed looks.

"Hey! You want the silver or not!" the merchant called after him, but Zhihao couldn't respond. He had to get to Jiayi. What if she was in trouble? Or someone was trying to kidnap her?

He finally rushed around a rather large man and found Jiayi standing near a stall of mostly embroidered shawls.

"Are you all right?" he asked, gripping her arm and looking at her to make sure she wasn't injured.

"You must buy that bracelet!" she said.

"What?" he asked her. She looked at a small silver bracelet on the table. "Why?" he asked. The bracelet did not look old, and was probably of foreign origin.

"As I walked past, I felt it...pulling me toward it," she said. "As though my hand wanted to reach out and touch it of its own accord."

"Are you sure?" he asked. "Has that ever happened before?"

She shook her head. "That is why I think there is something significant about it."

"A beautiful bracelet for a beautiful lady," the merchant said, picking up the trinket and reaching for Jiayi's hand.

Jiayi pulled away and shook her head. "I don't want to touch it here," she whispered to Zhihao.

"No need to be shy," the woman said. "Once you see it on, I am sure you will not be able to live without it."

"How much?" Zhihao asked, and he could see a greedy gleam in the woman's eye. Jiayi should not have shown so much interest in the bracelet. The seller knew how badly she wanted it.

"Oh, it is a very precious item," the woman said, trying to make it sound as valuable as possible. Zhihao sighed and crossed his arms. "It has a long history and is very important to me."

"Then why are you selling it?" Zhihao asked.

"Hard times make beggars of us all," the woman said. "But I will give you a good price."

In the end, Zhihao was certain he vastly overpaid for the bracelet, but Jiayi's eyes sparkled as he showed it to her.

"I hope the empress pays me back for this," he said.

Jiayi pulled back her sleeves and held her hands up to the bracelet, but she was far enough away that she could not actually touch it.

"It's incredible," she said. "I can practically feel heat coming off of it. Can't you feel that?"

"I don't feel anything," he said. "But has this happened before? You've never mentioned it."

She shook her head. "No. I don't know what is happening. But it must mean something, right?"

"I have no idea how your visions work," he said, placing the bracelet into her bag. "Maybe Hu Xiaosheng will know." He immediately regretted his words since they would no doubt encourage Jiayi to continue visiting the library.

"He is very wise," Jiayi said, looking thoughtfully into her bag for a moment and then closing it to continue walking through the market. "I am so fortunate to have him in my life."

Zhihao nodded. *Not nearly as fortunate as I am to have you in mine*, he thought, but then he shook his head. What was he doing? Jiayi didn't think of him that way. And the empress would never allow it. He was lucky that Jiayi consented to even be his friend and work with him. After all the stupid, hateful things he had said to her in the past, she would be right to refuse to have anything to do with him.

As they walked together, he couldn't help but watch the gentle way she walked and moved. The way her eyes lit up at seeing certain objects. How she listened with rapt attention as he explained what various items were. He knew that there was no better way to spend an afternoon than with her. Several men took note that the two of them were together and gave him approving nods as she passed them. He felt his chest puff up at all the men thinking that Jiayi was his wife.

He then remembered how Lian went on and on about claiming Jiayi for himself and he felt a gloom settle over him. Prince Kang had his eyes on her as well, he was sure of it. And Kang lived in the palace. Any time Kang wanted, he could see or talk to Jiayi...or do even more. Zhihao never imagined he would miss Eunuch Lo, but without her guardian, Jiayi had no one to protect her from Kang's advances—if she wanted to be protected from them.

He also remembered what Lian said about Kang possibly being a revolutionary. Or a spy. He wondered if Jiayi had noticed anything strange about Kang. Could she also be in danger if Kang was a spy? If Zhihao were implicated as a revolutionary for keeping company with Lian, so could Jiayi for spending so much time with him. He had to warn her to stay away from Kang.

"Jiayi," he said, "have you spoken to Prince Kang?"

She stopped suddenly. "What do you mean?" she asked.

He did not think there was any ambiguity in his question, but he pressed on. "After we met the prince during the audience the other day, have you spoken to him since then?"

"Yes," she said, but she did not seem eager to elaborate. He felt anger bubble up in him. Why would she be hedging if there was nothing to hide? Perhaps things with Kang had escalated between them already.

"What did you talk about?" he asked.

She scoffed and then frowned. "I don't think that's any of your business," she said.

"Don't be childish," he said. "Just tell me."

"No!" she said, walking away from him.

"Jiayi!" he called. "Come back here right now!" But Jiayi did not stop. She reached the end of the street, bought some joss sticks from a woman selling them out of a basket, and went through the temple gate.

Zhihao trotted to catch up with her as she was lighting one of the sticks and placing it in a large brazier in the temple courtyard.

"What are you doing?" he asked her.

"Praying for calm," she said as she closed her eyes and breathed through her nose.

"You don't need to be angry," Zhihao said. "I just asked you a question. Why can't you answer it?"

"Because it isn't your business," Jiayi said and she turned away, crossing the courtyard and flying up the stairs into the temple.

Inside the temple, a giant statue of a Buddha, the head of him almost touching the ceiling, took up the center of the room. There were a few monks and petitioners inside, but everyone spoke in low voices. Jiayi walked to the statue and placed her joss sticks into the offering trough in front of the statue, then she kneeled onto a cushion in front of it to pray.

Zhihao rolled his eyes and crossed his arms, waiting for her to finish. After several minutes, she still hadn't moved. When a cushion next to Jiayi became free, Zhihao rushed in front of a person who had clearly been waiting to pray to claim the spot. He heard the woman he had cut in front of gasp and say something under her breath, but he ignored her.

"Jiayi!" he hissed. "What are you doing? Let's go."

"Now you are going to dictate how much time I can spend praying?" she asked.

"I need to go back to work," he said.

"Then go," she said, her eyes closed and her hands folded in front of her. "I don't need you to wait for me. I can hire a rickshaw to take me back to the palace."

"I cannot leave you alone in the city!" he exclaimed. "If the empress found out, she would kill me."

"I won't tell her," Jiayi said, her voice as serene as a saint.

Zhihao stood up and grabbed Jiayi by the arm, forcing her to stand as well. "Enough. Let's go."

"Let me go!" she cried, pounding on his arm with one of her little fists.

Zhihao glanced around, but no one dared to intervene between what they thought was a dispute between a man and his wife.

"I'm trying to protect you!" he said.

"By hurting me?" she asked, tears filling her eyes.

Zhihao let her go and was suddenly ashamed of his actions as she rubbed where he had grabbed her so roughly.

"I'm sorry, Jiayi," he said, being sure to keep his voice

calm. "But I need you to listen to me. Kang could be dangerous."

"What do you know about him?" she yelled, paying no attention to the fact that they were in a temple.

"I heard a rumor that greatly disturbed me," he tried to explain.

"You would believe anything bad about him," Jiayi said. "Just because he was kind to me."

"What?" Zhihao asked.

"Sir," one of the monks said, interrupting them. "Madam." He then motioned toward the door, urging them to take their domestic squabble outside.

Zhihao reached for Jiayi to gently lead her outside, but she flinched and pulled away from him. Zhihao cursed to himself and moved toward the door, Jiayi not far behind.

"What did you mean?" he asked her again once they were in the courtyard.

Jiayi pushed past him toward the gate. "You were the same with Marcus," she said.

"Marcus?" he asked, keeping pace with her. "You are angry that I didn't like the man who tried to kidnap you into slavery?"

"You didn't know he was a slaver when we met him at the inn," Jiayi said. "You were just jealous that he thought I was pretty and complimented my English."

"That's not quite true," Zhihao said, even though he knew it was partly true—if not completely true. "I knew Marcus from my years in England. I knew he was a dangerous man."

"Do you know Prince Kang?" Jiayi asked, slowing her steps slightly.

"No," he admitted. "But a close friend of mine does. He told me something concerning about the prince."

"What?" she asked, stopping and looking at him.

"Well, it could be something," he said. "Or nothing."

"Tell me," she insisted.

"It is possible that the prince has revolutionary leanings," he said.

"But he's a prince," Jiayi said.

"That is what makes it so strange," Zhihao said. "I can't help but wonder if he is a spy, trying to find out the identities of other revolutionaries."

"But I'm not a revolutionary," Jiayi said. "Why would I be a danger?"

"Because you associate with me," he said.

Jiayi gasped and took a step back. "You are a revolutionary?" she asked in a hissing whisper.

"Shhh!" he said, trying to quiet her in the crowded market.

"But how could the empress not know already?" Jiayi asked. "She would never have hired you if she thought you had any anti-Manchu sentiment."

"I don't," he said. "Well...not as much as some people."

"But you have some," Jiayi said.

"I'm Han," he said. "Of course I support Chinese interests."

"But I'm Manchu," Jiayi said. "And so is Prince Kang."

"That doesn't matter," Zhihao said. "I have friends who are revolutionary. If Kang betrays my friends, I could get tangled up in it. And so could you."

"It does matter," Jiayi said.

"What?" Zhihao asked.

"The fact that I am Manchu does matter," she said, and he realized he had spoken without thinking again. "You spoke about Chinese interests. But what about my heritage?"

"The heritage that makes you a slave?" Zhihao asked. "Wouldn't you want to break free from that?"

"You know I want to be free," Jiayi said. "But no matter where I go, I will always be Manchu. That will never change."

Zhihao knew she was right. Even though it was legal for Han and Manchu to marry, the differences between their cultures were still vast.

"Come on," he said, motioning out of the market and toward a street where rickshaw pullers were waiting for riders. Jiayi followed, but she still did not allow him to touch her. "I need to get back to the library. But just listen to me. Stay away from Kang. Be careful what you say in his presence. And never be alone with him."

"If the prince is looking for revolutionaries," Jiayi said, "I think you are more of a danger to me than he is."

"Jiayi..." Zhihao said in a warning tone.

"Maybe you were right," she said as she climbed up into a rickshaw. "Maybe I should spend less time at the library. Less time with you."

"That is not what I meant and you know it," Zhihao said. "I am trying to help you. Keep you safe. I am still looking for a way to help you escape."

"Don't bother," Jiayi said. "Maybe I would be safer with my own people." She then told the driver to take her to the palace.

Zhihao jumped back to avoid the rickshaw wheels rolling over his toes. He cursed to himself again. It seemed he could not have a single conversation with Jiayi that did not end in a fight of some kind. And yet, he could not stay away from her. Could not stop thinking of her. He wanted to find some way for her to be in his life.

As he climbed into the next available rickshaw, he felt

the Tang Dynasty mirror in his pocket tap against his thigh. He had planned to give it to Jiayi today, not just to see if it belonged to Empress Wu, but as a gift. He would have to give it to her the next time he saw her—if she would ever agree to see him again.

SEVEN

*J*iayi was sitting at a stone table in one of the gardens, practicing writing her name. Unfortunately, she had to admit that Zhihao had been right. She was improving quickly. Even though she usually sketched with charcoal, writing with a brush was another form of art, and she found the process of bringing characters to life enjoyable. She had even strayed a bit from the "correct" way of making the characters by developing her own style. She would draw as many strokes as possible without lifting the brush from the paper. She experimented with different amounts of ink on the brush and varying the pressure she used. Every time she wrote her name, it looked a little different, and she enjoyed the challenge of making it more and more—

"Beautiful," Prince Kang said from over her shoulder.

Jiayi dropped her brush, which fell onto her skirt, leaving a black smear. But she ignored it as she fell to her knees to bow before the prince. She had been concentrating so deeply on her writing that she had not heard him approach.

The prince gasped and reached for her hand to pull her back to her feet. "Your gown!"

"It's nothing," she said.

"I'm sorry," he said, pulling an embroidered kerchief out of his pocket, wetting it in a nearby birdbath, and then reaching to wipe the ink from her gown.

"That kerchief is worth more than my hideous dress," she said. As she tried to stop him, their hands touched.

"Please," the prince said, "let me help."

She finally relented. After all, it was not her place to tell a prince what to do. The prince kneeled before her, dabbing at the spot with his kerchief. It was so strange to her to have a prince at her feet. Even Prince Junjie did not humble himself before Lady Meirong in such a way. She glanced around and saw some other ladies and eunuchs who were taking in the sun and fresh air of the garden looking at her and whispering behind their hands. What would the empress or Princess Der Ling think when they heard about this? Her heart began to race and she was glad when the prince finally finished and stood up.

"There," he said. "Not quite good as new, but it should not be noticeable now."

"Thank you," she said with a curtsey. "May I take your kerchief and clean it for you?"

He handed it to her with a smile. "Why don't you keep it?"

Even though it was now slightly stained, she knew it was an expensive gift, and she wondered if there was more significance to him giving to her than sheer politeness.

"You are too kind, Your Highness," she said.

He chuckled. "I am not sure I will ever get used to being called that. Would you do me the honor of calling me Little Wolf instead?"

"Little Wolf?" she asked.

"It was the name my family called me," he said. "I rather miss it. The empress named me Kang. She thought it sounded more regal. And if I am ever emperor, I know I will be given another name. It's all a lot to keep track of, and none of it feels like me."

Jiayi nodded. She understood the feeling of losing hold of your own identity. She spent so much time in the bodies of other people, she sometimes wondered how much she was really herself or simply cobbled together from the thoughts of others.

"When I was a child, I was called Sparrow," Jiayi said.

"Would you like me to call you Sparrow?" Kang asked.

Jiayi shook her head. "That was another life."

"If you called me Little Wolf, it would be a great comfort," Kang explained.

Jiayi shook her head. "You know I cannot. It would be disrespectful. I would be punished if anyone heard me."

"Perhaps only when we are alone, then," he whispered. "Like right now." She blushed and looked away, and he laughed. He reached out and tugged on her elbow. "Come, say it."

She hesitated, looking around to make sure no one was within listening range, even though she could still see people watching them from a distance. She hid her mouth behind her sleeve.

"Little Wolf," she whispered.

"I can't hear you," he said, leaning in a little closer.

"You are going to get me into trouble...Little Wolf," she said, and he burst into laughter. She giggled, still hiding her mouth behind her sleeve.

"I have not been called that in months," he said with a sigh. "Thank you."

"You never need to thank me for anything," she said. "I am just a servant."

"When I am emperor," he said, "you will be far more than that. I will elevate you to Great Lady."

"What?" she asked with a laugh, thinking he was joking. "What a silly thing to say."

"Not at all!" he replied. "You have a marvelous gift. I would be honored for you to be one of my advisors."

Jiayi gasped, her hand flying to her chest. "An advisor? Now you are surely telling fibs."

"Do you not know how much my aunt depends on your counsel?" he asked her.

She shook her head. "After I have a vision for her, she sends me away. She has never spoken to me beyond ordering me to touch this or that."

"Well, she might not make it clear to you, but she speaks of you and your words often," he said. "Most of her decisions are based on your visions in some capacity."

Jiayi turned away, confused by his words. "But...why?" she asked.

"Do you know how she plans to make me emperor?" he asked.

"Something about using Empress Wu to...displace the young emperor," she said in a whisper.

"Exactly," he said. "The empress is old, and her health is growing more precarious. She fears for the future of her country. Even though you found the seal, it does not seem to have been enough to create confidence in the emperor. If anything, it made the people doubt him more since he, his cousin, and his great-uncle before him all ruled without the Mandate of Heaven."

Jiayi shook her head. She had no idea that finding the

seal had made matters worse for the empress. No wonder she had not softened toward Jiayi.

"The current emperor will not be able to remain in control over the Han should the empress die," Kang continued. "He is weak. Malleable. He is like a willow, bending whichever way the wind blows. She must become empress in her own right and appoint me as her heir before it is too late. I can help restore Han confidence in the Manchu. The empress believes you are the only person who can get me on the throne."

"But I don't know how," Jiayi said.

"Find the items belonging to Empress Wu," he said. "She believes the answer is there."

Jiayi felt a hitch in her chest as she remembered the empress's dagger in Der Ling's possession.

"What if I fail?" Jiayi asked.

The prince smirked. "I suggest you don't."

Jiayi's face fell. She did not see the humor in is words. She had always been fearful of the empress. This new knowledge concerned her even more. If the empress was in ill health, it could make her temperament even shorter. Jiayi could be running out of time to either find a way to help the empress depose the emperor or escape.

The prince must have seen the concern on her face. He reached out and placed a hand on her shoulder. Even though his touch was light, the significance of the motion felt heavy as a boulder to Jiayi. "I beg of you not to worry, dear Jiayi," he said. "I will do whatever I can to help you. All anyone can ask is that you try your best. But should you be in need of aid, I will protect you."

"Why?" Jiayi asked without thinking.

"Isn't it obvious?" he asked, and she felt her heart flutter. No man had ever been so kind to her when she was awake before. He certainly could not be saying what she thought he was saying...could he? Could a prince, a possible future emperor, have feelings for her? A lowly servant? A slave even? A girl from the streets who could not write her own name?

She shook her head. "I don't understand. I'm too stupid—"

"Never say that in my presence again," the prince ordered. "You are brilliant, Jiayi. The most special woman in the world. No one else can do what you do. Any man—any person—any *empress*—who cannot see your true worth is a fool."

Jiayi felt her face flush and her heart race. She couldn't breathe. It was too much. Why was he saying these things? He couldn't mean them. Yes, she had strange powers. But they had not made her life better. If anything, they imperiled her life. If she had never been sold to the empress, she would at least be free. She could have stayed with her family. She might have married. She wondered, if she ever escaped, if she could keep her powers hidden. Live a new life without anyone knowing what she was capable of. Live a normal life.

She thought about what Zhihao said, about Prince Kang being dangerous. A revolutionary or a spy. She didn't think he was right about that. But the prince could be endangering her in some other way. If the empress knew what he had been telling her, she might be furious. And Der Ling. She had her own plans for Jiayi's powers. Jiayi wanted to think of Der Ling as a friend. Someone who might have the authority to help her. She didn't want to betray the princess.

"I...I have to go," she finally said, rushing away. She felt the prince reach for her arm, but she slipped from his grasp. She needed to get away. Be alone. Find somewhere safe.

Somewhere that no one would try to use her for their own gains. She left her writing tools behind as she rushed to her room, shutting and locking the door behind her.

She slipped to the floor and tried to pry up the board that guarded her treasures, but her eyes were filled with tears and her fingers wouldn't cooperate. She wasn't sure why she was crying. The prince had been so kind. So encouraging. Gentle even.

She slapped her hand on the panel and then leaned against a nearby wall. Was it possible the prince had feelings for her? Would he really keep her safe? What did he mean by that? Was it possible he would take her as a consort? It was not unheard of for emperors to take consorts from among palace maids. That was why all maids had to be Manchu women. There could be no possibility of an emperor taking a Han woman as a consort. But the empress would probably never allow Kang to take her as a consort. But if the empress died...He did say that her health was failing. If the empress could depose the emperor, appoint Kang as her heir, and then die, it would be within Kang's power and right to make Jiayi a consort.

Perhaps life as a consort would not be a terrible fate. She had always dreamed of escaping the Forbidden City. But what if the answer to her problems had presented itself right here—in the guise of Little Wolf.

She snorted and shook her head, wiping the tears from her eyes. Why couldn't Zhihao be that nice to her? He was always so mean. So rude. Except when he wasn't. He was the first person to believe in her. The person who gave her hope. He was the only man she had imagined possibly having a life with other than Prince Junjie...

No, it was stupid. No one would ever marry her. The prince would have to marry a noblewoman. Zhihao would find a wealthy Han woman from a good family. Someone smart. Educated. Elegant. A Chinese version of Rebecca, the woman he had loved in England.

But then again, Empress Wu had once been a nun. A woman forbidden to marry or even leave her temple. Her situation must have seemed even more hopeless than Jiayi's. How could a nun ever hope to escape her situation? And that she eventually became empress was astonishing. Maybe Jiayi could learn a thing or two from Empress Wu herself.

At that, Jiayi remembered the strange bracelet Zhihao had bought for her in the marketplace. She had planned to touch it the next time she and Zhihao were together so she could tell him whatever she learned. She went to the bag where she had left the bracelet. She covered her hands with her sleeves as she pulled it out. She sat on the bed, examining it in the low light of her room.

It seemed simple enough. The silver had mostly tarnished to black, but she could still make out the etchings of a dragon and phoenix on the outside—similar to Lady Meirong's necklace she used to visit Prince Junjie—and elegant scrollwork etched on the inside. She thought that it must have been a rather expensive piece in its time for the silversmith to have bothered carving the inside as well.

Jiayi took a deep breath and threw back one of her sleeves. She reached toward the bracelet, but she could feel the power it exuded before she even touched it. Her hand simply hovered over the bracelet for a moment, and she could feel something like tingling in her fingertips.

Suddenly, she was kneeling with her forehead to the floor.

"Worthless little pig!" someone screeched.

She looked up and gasped when she saw Empress Wu glaring back at her.

"How dare you look at me!" the empress snapped just before she slapped Jiayi, sending her falling backward.

"I...I..." Jiayi scrambled to make sense of what was happening. She looked down and saw that she was dressed as a Tang Dynasty maid. She had never been a maid in this era before, but she had seen them plenty of times when she had been Lady Meirong. But how was she even here? She hadn't touched the bracelet.

"Get up!" the empress screamed, and Jiayi resumed her kneeling position on the floor.

"I am sorry, Your Majesty," she said. "Forgive me!" She had no idea what she was apologizing for. But she was sure that, like all maids, she had been blamed for some slight that was not her fault.

The empress then swept her arm across the dressing table she was sitting at, sending jars of face paints, powders, scents, jewelry, and hair decorations crashing to the floor around Jiayi.

Jiayi covered her head with her hands to protect herself from the glass that shattered around her.

"Look what you made me do!" Empress Wu said.

"I am so clumsy!" Jiayi said.

The empress stood and stomped across the room. "Clean this up before I return!" she shouted as she slammed the door shut.

Jiayi waited for a moment before moving, just in case the empress came back. Once she was sure she was alone, she sat up and surveyed her surroundings. She was in Empress Wu's room, and the woman had been quite young. She would not have been empress yet, but a second-rank concubine.

Jiayi stood up and began raking up the glass with her hands. She winced as the glass poked her delicate skin, making small scratches that bled. But she continued to work. She knew that if the empress returned and the mess was still here, she would be even more furious.

As she picked up an overturned jewelry box, the silver bracelet she was holding in her hand in her waking life tumbled out. It was no longer tarnished, but shone brightly, the magnificent craftsmanship of the silver clearly visible.

She picked up the bracelet and turned it around in her hands. She slipped it onto her delicate wrist and admired how lovely it looked on her. Why had the bracelet sent her here? Why did it seem to call to her? After a moment, when nothing happened, she sighed and placed the bracelet back into the box and put it on Empress's Wu's dressing table. She finished cleaning up the mess, salvaging whatever makeup or powders she could and discarding whatever was ruined.

When she was done, Empress Wu still had not returned, so she went to the door to leave the room. As she did, she thought about the bracelet in the box. She opened the door to make sure no one was coming, then she ducked back inside, closing the door firmly behind her.

Jiayi went to the closet where the empress kept her gowns and other jewels. She rummaged through the various items until she found another silver bracelet. It wasn't as lovely as the first bracelet, but since the empress had so many, she was certain the woman would not take note of the slight differences. Jiayi then went to the dressing table and swapped out the bracelets.

When she tried to slip the dragon and phoenix bracelet into her waistband, though, her hand froze. Her heart skipped a beat. What was happening? She looked to the door, but she was still alone. Her vision was still clear and she was not having trouble breathing. She then tried to move her hand again, but could not.

"No," a voice said inside her head. "Danger."

"Who...who is that?" Jiayi asked, but there was no reply. She used all her strength to force her hand to move. Slowly, she slipped the dragon and phoenix bracelet into the waistband of her skirt and smoothed her top over it. She looked in the mirror of the table to make sure the bracelet was not visible. It had been a while since she had stolen something, and she could not deny that she felt a bit of excitement bubbling in her stomach. Besides, was she really stealing? The bracelet obviously wanted her to take it. It needed to tell her something. How could it do that if she left it behind?

She smirked to herself as she realized she was controlling the maid's actions. It was the maid who was trying to stop her from stealing. The maid speaking to her in her mind. But Jiayi was stronger. Jiayi was no longer being swept along through time. She was making a change.

This had to be why the bracelet had called to her. To teach her how to change the past. Her heart raced. This was what she had been working toward. If she could control her host, she could save Prince Junjie!

She smiled and looked at herself in the mirror, but when she saw her face, she nearly screamed. She was looking at herself! She leaned forward to get a closer look at her reflection. In all the hundreds of visions she had ever had, she had never retained her own face before. She touched her cheeks and her chin and noticed some subtle differences. This woman's skin was darker, and she was even thinner than Jiayi, her cheeks sunken in a bit. So, it was not Jiayi. Not really. But the similarities were unnerving.

She stood and rushed to the door, wanting to get out before the empress returned and away from the face in the mirror.

As she slipped into the hall and closed the door behind her, she was back in her own bed, the silver bracelet still lying in her hand, protected by the sleeve of her gown. She shook her head, trying to understand what had happened. Her other hand must have been closer to the bracelet than she realized. She must have touched it, inciting the vision.

She laughed to herself. She had just stolen from Empress Wu. She closed her eyes and imagined what she would change the next time she saw Prince Junjie.

EIGHT

Zhihao was disgusted with himself. He could barely look at his face in the mirror as he dressed, which made shaving a particularly painful process. He cursed as he cut his jaw, which dripped a spot of blood onto his shirt. He did his best to wipe the blood away, but the spot remained. He finally tossed the shirt into a basket for his mother to deal with and got out a new one. But as he buttoned up the clean shirt, he still felt the stain of how he had treated Jiayi the day before.

How could he have been so rough with her? She was a delicate woman. He hoped he had not bruised her arm. He had been a brute, and he would not be surprised if she never wanted to see him again.

He couldn't figure out why he had been angry. Jiayi was precious to him. She was smart and talented. He loved looking at the charcoal drawings she had made of her visions. She was the reason he was making a name for himself in the world of archeology. As Lian had said, she would not be the sort of wife who would only sit at home, waiting for him to pay her a little bit of attention. She could be a partner. A friend. A wife he could love and respect. She was also beautiful, a fact he could not deny, but it was not the only reason he wanted to be near her.

But he had hurt her. Scared her. He regularly insulted her. He knew that many wives, including his own mother, put up with much worse from the men in their lives. His father had not been one to temper his anger, often doling out physical punishments to his mother and sisters if they ran afoul of Father's wishes.

But Jiayi was different. Mainly in the fact that she wasn't his wife. They were partners. Working together to fulfill the whims of the empress. Even though the empress herself often physically punished Jiayi, if she knew that Zhihao had laid a hand on her, he most likely would find himself with one less hand, if not one less head.

He realized that if he ever wanted to be more than just a friend to Jiayi, he might have to actually court her. He almost laughed at that. Courting was not something that most men did. Marriages were arranged. Men often had just as little say in their unions as women did. But he had spent his formative years in England. And when he was of an age that he first started noticing women, he also learned to be polite and courteous. He opened doors, pulled out chairs, and bought them flowers. If Rebecca saw the way he had been treating Jiayi, she would have been mortified.

Not that he had any reason to think that he would ever be able to court Jiayi. Or that she would want him to. He still had no plan to secret her out of the country. America was off-limits to women. He had visited the British consulate, but without an invitation for gainful employment, he could not obtain visas there either. He also did not want to leave his mother. He did not think the empress would allow him to marry Jiayi, but he could not steal her away without a plan for leaving China.

In a way, they were both trapped.

But at least he could start trying to repair and build a positive relationship with Jiayi. He had no class this morning, so he was going to the Forbidden City to see Jiayi and apologize. They could then perhaps visit another market and find more Tang era items. He was anxious to know what the bracelet might have in store for her. Whether it was actually "calling" to her or not, he had no idea. He had no idea how her visions worked; he could only take her word for it. But she had wanted it badly. There must have been a reason.

He also wanted to give her the mirror he had bought for her. It wasn't flowers, but given Jiayi's powers, he hoped it would be a more meaningful gift for her.

Just as he picked up his hat and jacket, there was a knock at his door, then his mother entered without waiting for a reply.

"I'm just leaving," he said. "Wash that shirt quickly; there is a stain on the collar."

"I'll have the maid do it," she said as she tottered into the room, leaning on her cane to alleviate the pressure on her bound feet.

"No!" he moaned. "She never takes as much care as you do. She will let it sit until it is ruined."

"Fine, fine," she said as she waved a piece of paper at him. "This letter arrived for you."

He tried to grab it, but she snatched it away.

"What?" he asked.

"Zhihao," she said, using her serious tone, "I know everything you were doing when you were at school. Don't think that just because you were so far away, I didn't know about that British girl you carried on with."

"That's in the past, Ma," Zhihao said. "I don't want to talk about her anymore. What does this have to do with—"

His stomach felt sick as his mother showed him the envelope. In Rebecca's signature scrolling penmanship that he would recognize anywhere, Zhihao saw his English name, Theodore, written alongside his Chinese name and address. One thing that had always impressed him about her was her easy command of languages.

But why was she writing to him now? They hadn't spoken in years. They were barely able to retain their relationship back in England after Eli's death. And after he returned to China, they never spoke again.

He could not deny that he had often thought about writing to her. In the first year he was home, he had put pen to paper nearly every day. But after "Dear Rebecca," the words fell away and he was unable to continue. Eventually, he came to accept that they were from two different worlds and that it had been better for them to go their separate ways.

He knew, though, that had this letter arrived at any time before he met Jiayi, he would have ripped it open eagerly. Now, he only stared at the envelope, as if he was afraid that just by touching it, it might throw his whole world into disarray.

"Get rid of it," he said.

His mother cocked her eyebrow, as though asking if he was sure.

"Yes, burn it," he said. "And any others that arrive. I'm going to the Forbidden City today."

"Fine," his mother said, trying to hide the giddiness in her voice. She most likely had been even more frightened of the letter's contents than he was. The idea of her son marrying a foreign girl was a terrifying concept. Some of Zhihao's classmates had actually married British wives. Some stayed in England, but a few had returned to China and tried to integrate their wives into their families, often resulting in the woman returning to England a few weeks later, never to be heard from again. Of course, the families were never allowed to forget the disgrace their sons caused, and it was difficult for the men to remarry. No one wanted their own daughter to be a second wife after a foreigner.

Zhihao rushed out of the house and jumped into the first rickshaw he could find, as if the dreaded letter might chase after him.

Zhihao paced the long audience hall where he usually met with the empress. But he was not waiting for the empress for once. He had asked a eunuch to tell Jiayi that he was here to see her.

He wasn't quite sure what he was going to say when he saw her. Everything he practiced in his head felt woefully inadequate. He was mumbling to himself, trying to come up with just the right words when he heard footsteps across the hall. He turned, but the smile ran from his face when he saw Prince Kang walking toward him.

"Zhihao Shaoye!" Prince Kang said, smiling and holding his hand outstretched.

Zhihao cursed to himself. He couldn't believe the gods were already testing his resolve to act less boorish. He forced a smile to his face and grasped Kang's offered hand.

"Your Highness," he then said, offering a bow.

"My friend," the prince said, "have you found any

market treasures? I would be most interested to know how you select items. How do you know if something is ancient or just a cheap copy?"

"That is an excellent question, Your Highness," Zhihao said. "But it is a skill I have spent many years training. I have studied much of the art and culture of times past to know what I am looking for."

"Fantastic," the prince said, and Zhihao couldn't help but smile a bit. The prince seemed just as easily impressed as Jiayi. "Perhaps I could go to the market with you. See you use this incredible skill."

"Only if you dress like a peasant," Zhihao said. "If you dress like a prince, the sellers will refuse to make me a good bargain."

Kang laughed and slapped Zhihao on the shoulder. Zhihao laughed as well and could not deny that the prince was an easily likable man. But then he remembered what Lian had told him, and his own warnings to Jiayi. The prince seemed to be someone who could put people at ease. Gain their trust. Maybe that was how he had been able to infiltrate the revolutionary groups. Or perhaps he was a genuine person and did have revolutionary leanings. But if that were true, why was he here? Though Zhihao had to admit, trying to depose the emperor and take his place was a radical undertaking. Maybe the prince was a revolutionary after all.

Thankfully, Jiayi showed up at that moment, saving him from having to continue the conversation with the prince on his own.

He smiled at her as she walked toward him, swaying carefully on her pot-bottom shoes. Out of the corner of his eye, he also noticed Prince Kang was admiring her, and his jealousy bloomed like a mold spore on a damp wall. He did his best to tamp his anger down. He could not fail in his new resolve before he had even started.

Jiayi reached them and bent at the knees, lowering her head in a bow. "Prince Kang. Zhihao."

"Jiayi," Prince Kang said, pleading with her, "what did I say to call me?"

Zhihao clenched his teeth together as he waited for her answer. She glanced at him and then looked away, keeping her eyes lowered.

"Only in private," she whispered.

Zhihao wanted to explode. The prince had asked her to call him something else in private? Some sort of pet name? A term of endearment? What was it?

But the prince laughed. Did the man never take anything seriously?

"Jiayi!" the prince said. "Zhihao is a friend. He will not tell the empress you have been impertinent. Right, Zhihao?" The prince then slapped him on the back, this time causing him to cough.

"R-r-right," he sputtered.

"See!" the prince said, turning back to Jiayi. "We are all in good company."

"Of course," Jiayi said, but she hesitated before adding in an even smaller voice, "Little Wolf."

The prince chucked Jiayi under the chin. "Was that so hard, my girl?" he asked.

His girl? Zhihao could hardly stand another moment. If Kang opened his mouth again, he might just find himself missing a tooth or two.

"Your Highness," Zhihao finally said, trying his best not to yell, "I have urgent business I must discuss with Jiayi, if you don't mind."

"No, I don't mind at all," the prince said. He made no move to leave.

"Alone," Zhihao finally said after an awkward minute.

"Oh," the prince said, not bothering to hide his disappointment. "Very well. Do send for me when you are done. The empress has been hounding me about your progress."

"Of course," Zhihao said, and he breathed much more easily as he watched the man leave the room.

When he turned back to Jiayi, he realized that he was the only person who felt relief at the prince's exit. She looked at him as though she was afraid he might strike her, and it caused great grief in his heart.

"Jiayi," he said as gently as possible. "I must apologize for my actions yesterday. I was a brute. I should not have treated you that way. I am sorry."

He saw her shoulders relax a bit.

"Thank you," she said stiffly.

"But not just yesterday," he continued. "I have often said cruel, thoughtless things to you. And while I have apologized before, this is not a conversation we should keep having. I am going to do my best to do better in the future, I promise you."

Jiayi said nothing, so he kept going.

"You are very dear to me. I value your friendship and the work we do together. I know you think you are a slave because of the empress, and your background, and your lack of education. But you are not. You are a smart, talented, beautiful lady. And if I ever again treat you as less than the lady you are, I hope you will take me to task for it. And I—"

"Stop," she said, raising her hand. He felt his face go hot. Indeed, he had started to ramble.

"Thank you," she said again, but this time with more conviction. "I accept your apology."

He smiled and sighed with relief. He fished around in his pocket for the mirror, which his mother had cleaned and buffed so it shone like new. He pulled it out and offered it to her.

"I bought this for you," he said.

She looked at it, but did not reach out to take it.

"For me?" she asked. "You mean to touch for the empress?"

"Sort of," he said. "It is from the Tang era, I believe. But if it did not belong to Empress Wu and there is nothing special for you to tell the empress about it, I hope you will keep it for yourself." He turned it over. "It is a mirror, see?"

Jiayi reached out with her long sleeves covering her hands and took the mirror. She held it up and looked at her reflection.

"It is beautiful," she said.

"Not as beautiful as you," he replied.

Jiayi looked up at him in shock, her eyes wide. Then her face turned pink and she looked away.

"W-w-why would you say that?" she asked.

"Because it is true," he replied, reaching out and touching her cheek.

"No!" she said, stepping back. "Someone could see. Someone is always watching."

"Of course," Zhihao said, firmly placing his arms by his side.

"But...what are you doing?" she asked. "We have barely been friends. You just admitted that you have been very unkind to me in the short time we have known each other. And now...what? You are...seducing me?"

"What?" Zhihao asked. "No! I would never put you in a compromising position."

"Then why were you complimenting me like that?" she asked.

"Because, Jiayi, I care for you...deeply," he tried to explain. "I would take you away from here if I could. I would marry you."

Jiayi gasped, her sleeved hand flying to her mouth.

"I haven't forgotten my promise to help you," he said. "I have been looking for options. I went to the British consulate to ask about visas, but they couldn't help me. And there is also my mother. I can't abandon her. But I didn't want you to think I was content to let you stay here in service to the empress."

Jiayi turned away, and for a moment, he was afraid she was going to run. He often forgot how much she could act like a startled rabbit if he weren't careful.

"Have I upset you?" he asked. "That was not my intention."

"No...," she said, but she did not elaborate. Something was clearly worrying her.

"Then what is wrong?" he asked. "You can tell me." He stepped around her so she would have to face him again.

"I...I can't," she said, shaking her head.

He felt a sinking feeling inside. "Why not?" he asked. "Is it because you don't feel the same way? Is there someone else?" He hesitated but then forced himself to ask, "Is it Kang?"

"No," she said, a hint of annoyance in her voice. But then she seemed to remember something. "At least, not in the way you think."

"How could it be any other way than what I am thinking right now?" Zhihao asked. "Has he asked you to be his lover? Or consort? Made promises of marriage if you help him become emperor?"

Jiayi sighed and shook her head. "He hasn't said anything of the sort. But things here are complicated. Everyone wants something from me."

"Has he threatened you?" Zhihao asked. "Do you think he is a spy?"

"No, he has not threatened me," Jiayi said.

"Then why can't you tell me?" Zhihao asked. "I just told you that I want to marry you. Why can't you be honest with me?"

"You asked me to marry you after months of treating me like dirt on your shoe," she said. "I do care for you. I'm just confused. I need time. I have a life here. Have been making my own plans for the future."

"What plans?" Zhihao asked.

"Stop asking me questions!" she finally snapped. "Please!"

The only response he had to that was to ask her why, but since she said to stop asking questions, he closed his mouth instead. He turned away and paced a bit. He was even more confused now than he was before. He did not regret apologizing, but perhaps he should not have mentioned marriage. It was a lot for him to lay at her feet so suddenly. He certainly was out of practice with this courtship thing.

He turned back to her, wanting to ask what he should do next, but that was another question, so again, he only pressed his lips shut, literally biting his tongue to keep quiet.

"Thank you," Jiayi finally said, holding up the mirror in her sleeved hand, "for the gift."

"It was my pleasure," he said.

"Would you like me to touch it?" she asked. "See if I can learn anything from it?"

"If you like," he said.

Jiayi kneeled on the floor and tossed back one of her sleeves. She held her hand over the mirror and let it hover for a moment like she had with the bracelet at the marketplace. She then took a deep breath, closed her eyes, and touched the mirror. But she didn't slump over. After a moment, she opened her eyes and looked around as though surprised to still be in the same place.

"Nothing," she said.

"Nothing?" he asked, forgetting he wasn't supposed to ask questions.

She shook her head. "I have the sense that it is old, but there is no memory in it. Perhaps it was never purchased. Or it was placed in a tomb when it was new, so the owner never had memories with it."

"Or it was owned by a man," Zhihao said. "Didn't you say you only ever took the form of a woman in your visions."

"That is possible," she said.

"Well, at least you don't have to worry about keeping it from the empress," he said. "It is just a gift."

"A fine gift," she said, standing. "I'll be able to use it without worrying about falling into the past."

Zhihao then cleared his throat and looked around. He supposed he had long overstayed his welcome.

"I should leave," he said.

"Wait," she said. "Not just yet. The bracelet."

"Oh, did you touch it?" he asked. "Learn something useful?"

"I did touch it," she said. "And I saw Empress Wu."

NINE

*J*iayi rushed to her room, at least as well as she could in her platform shoes. She was flustered and her face was flushed. What had gotten into Zhihao? He just did everything short of declaring love for her. Though, she didn't know anyone who married for love. Marriage was typically a necessity, to strengthen power or increase fortune. But what could she offer Zhihao? They did work well together. But wouldn't he want her to stay home and have children like all good wives? She supposed she could do that. There was no reason she should not be able to have children. She had never really thought about it. She did not imagine the empress would ever arrange a match for her, so she had not dared to dream of a life beyond service. Did she want children? Didn't all women? Though not all women were like her. What if she could pass her abilities on to her offspring? Would she want to subject them to such a life?

As she walked through the various courtyards and buildings to go to her small room at the back of the servants' quarters, she noticed several women watch her as she passed. They wrinkled their noses and whispered behind their sleeves. She held up her hand to the side of her face to avoid looking at them. She had no idea why they were staring. She must look a fright with her puffy eyes and flushed cheeks, practically running through the palace grounds.

She was already breathless by the time she reached her room, but after grabbing the bracelet, she now had to venture all the way back to the audience hall.

As she rounded a corner, she saw Prince Kang walking with the empress, along with all of the empress's followers of ladies and eunuchs. She ducked back behind the building and rushed in another direction before taking an alternate path. She prayed she had not been spotted.

She had not even had a chance to think about Prince Kang in all of Zhihao's wild rambling. Well, she had thought about how she had promised to help him become emperor, which made her remember her promise to help Der Ling. If Zhihao did find a way to take her away, could she just leave without fulfilling her promises? She supposed she could leave Der Ling, but Prince Kung...Little Wolf— her feelings about him were less clear. She did believe he would be a better emperor than the current one. A stronger emperor would be better for all of China. By helping Little Wolf, she could help everyone. It was a noble calling. It could be selfish of her to abandon her country and her people when she could help them.

And what if Little Wolf wanted more from her than just to be made emperor? He had been kind to her. Affectionate, even. She was certain that he had been hinting toward making her one of his consorts. Even a level seven consort would be a life of luxury she had never dared to dream of. Her own palace. Beautiful gowns. All the food she could ever eat. Servants to wait on her hand and foot. And if she was blessed to have a son, she could be the mother of the next emperor.

She scoffed and laughed at herself. What was she thinking? She would never be a consort. Much less an empress-mother. Kang was just being friendly. It was his way. Even Zhihao seemed less offended by Kang's presence when she arrived at the audience hall. He was probably just flattering her so she would use her powers for his advantage. He wanted to use treason to become emperor! A man with ambitions like that could never be fully trusted.

Her mind was still swirling when she made her way back to the audience hall.

"What took so long?" Zhihao asked.

"I had to take another path back to avoid Li—Prince Kang," she said.

Zhihao pressed his lips to keep from saying something and then cleared his throat. "Probably wise," he decided on. "So, what is so special about the bracelet."

"I'm not exactly sure," Jiayi said. "But when I touched it, I learned that it was indeed owned by Empress Wu. It was on her dressing table. But I wasn't the empress. I was her maid."

"I suppose it is to be expected that you could take the body of any woman who came into contact with the item," he said. "Perhaps you will be the empress next time."

"That is possible," Jiayi said. "But I still think the bracelet is trying to tell me something. If it is, why would it send me to the body of the maid?"

"You will just have to keep trying," Zhihao said. "You can only stay under for so long, as long as you hold your breath. It might take several tries for you to fully understand its importance."

Jiayi nodded, but she did not explain that her powers seemed to be getting stronger. That she could stay in them longer than she could hold her breath or even go under without completely touching the item. She wasn't sure what was happening or what she was fully capable of, so until she knew more, she thought it was better to keep the details to herself.

"Shall we try here?" Zhihao asked, motioning to the floor of the audience hall.

"No," Jiayi said. "We should go somewhere more private."

"W-w-what do you mean?" Zhihao stammered, and Jiayi thought she saw his face flush a little. What did he think she was referring to?

"Anyone could come upon us at any moment," she said. "I don't like to be a spectacle if I can avoid it." Even though most of her visions were held in front of a large audience of the empress and her followers, she hated feeling like an acrobat on display.

"Where shall we go?" Zhihao asked.

"Follow me," she said, and she led the way out the side door of the audience hall, after she took a moment to make sure no one was watching them. Of course, in the Forbidden City, someone was always watching. But if they were able to go to a more private location, at least fewer people would probably be watching. She did not want to be completely alone with Zhihao anyway. It would be highly improper, and the empress could have both of them severely punished. In a way, she missed Eunuch Lo. She didn't like how he was always with her, but if he was monitoring her, at least she could not be accused of wanton behavior.

She took Zhihao from the audience hall and down

several paths. They eventually ended up at The Palace of Heavenly Unity. Behind it was another small building, the Hall of Contemplation, where there were several places for sitting, talking, and drinking tea. The building was not a very popular place for gathering because it was shaded, often too cool, and had only one entrance. While the windows were latticed, so anyone would be able to look inside, their vision would be obscured.

"We should be allowed to talk here," Jiayi said, sitting at one side of a low tea table. Zhihao sat across from her. She held the bracelet in her sleeved hand.

"What happened when you touched the bracelet before?" Zhihao asked. "You said you were the empress's maid, but you did not say what you did."

"I stole this bracelet from her," Jiayi said, and Zhihao's jaw dropped.

"That seems rather significant," he said. "Why did you... she...the maid do that?"

"She didn't," Jiayi said. "The maid wanted to leave it on the empress's dressing table. I could feel her fighting me as I slipped the bracelet into my skirt and left the room."

"Why?" Zhihao asked. "How? I didn't think you could influence the person you were inhabiting."

"I've been practicing," she said. "Empress Wu was cruel to the maid. She struck me and threw her pots of face paint at me. So, when she was called away, I stole the bracelet from her."

Zhihao rubbed his jaw. "Jiayi, this sounds very dangerous. What if you had been caught?"

"But I wasn't," Jiayi said. "I slipped out of the room and woke up."

"But you left the maid behind," Zhihao said. "What if she was caught?"

"I hid it very well," Jiayi said, but she did feel a little twist in the pit of her stomach.

"Well, maybe it didn't happen how you think," he said. "You can't really change the past...can you?"

Not yet, Jiayi wanted to say, but she only shook her head. "No. I never have. You are right. After I left, I am sure everything happened the way it did before."

She turned the bracelet over in her hand, feeling the heat from it through the thin material of her sleeve. It wanted her to return. There was something else the bracelet needed her to see.

"Are you sure you should touch it?" Zhihao asked. "Something about this item seems different. You are acting differently. Your visions are different. Maybe it is dangerous."

"No, I must try," she said, "at least once more. I really think it is trying to tell me something important."

"Fine," Zhihao said. "But just take a short breath so you won't be gone long. And if anything goes wrong, just wake up."

"I will," she said, and she touched the bracelet.

*J*iayi was in terrible pain. She could barely even open her eyes as every part of her seemed to throb. She was being rocked back and forth and could hear people screaming at her. Finally, she raised her head to look around, but she could only open one eye. The other was swollen shut. The light was blinding, as though she had not seen the sun in days. She tried to raise her hand to shield her eyes, but her arms were bound fast behind her.

She cried out as she realized she was in an iron cage being rolled forward by a donkey. She was on her knees in a filthy gown covered in foul-smelling muck. The people around her shook their fists and threw cold and rotten food at her. Up ahead, she could see a raised platform—and an executioner holding a long sword.

"No!" she gasped as she realized she was being dragged to her death. The maid must have been caught after all and was about to be publicly executed for the crime. Jiayi had never died in one of her visions before. She had no idea if a death in a dream could lead to her death in real life—and she had no desire to find out.

As the donkey stopped, the iron cage lurched and she lost her balance, falling forward. The door of the cart was pulled open and a man grabbed at her ankle. Jiayi pulled her foot back and tried to scoot as far away from the man as possible.

"This is a mistake!" she said.

"Get over here!" the man said, leaping toward her and managing to get ahold of her leg. She screamed as her skin scraped against the bottom of the cart. She twisted and flailed, wanting to grab ahold of something, but her hands were bound fast.

As the man nearly dropped her to the ground, she more acutely felt the pains throughout her body. She had been beaten, starved, tortured, and raped.

"I'm sorry," she cried, hoping the maid could hear her. "I...I didn't mean for this to happen."

A bystander splashed a bowl of cold noodles and soup into her face as she reached the steps to the platform. She froze in shock, but the man escorting her pushed her, causing her to trip on the lowest step and slam her arm into the wooden beams. He then grabbed her by her bound arm and jerked her to her feet, practically dragging her up the stairs.

Once she was on the platform, the people began to cheer. How could they be so happy to see a young woman put to death?

Jiayi looked around, trying to figure out what to do or say. Some way to escape. But there was no way out. The platform was surrounded by an angry mob calling for her blood. On the platform, the guard blocked the stairs, the executioner stood ready with his sword, and the Minister of Justice, who she recognized by his tall hat, motioned for her to step forward.

She took small steps, her feet aching from the soles being beaten with bamboo rods.

"Song Jier," the minister said, reading from a scroll. "For the crime of stealing from her Imperial Majesty, impertinence, and willful disobedience, you have been sentenced to death by beheading. What have you to say for yourself?"

Her one good eye blurred with tears as she choked out, "I want to wake up."

The few people in the front of the crowd who could hear her laughed and the minister shook his head sadly.

"Soon you will sleep with your ancestors," he said, "but I doubt they will welcome a wicked girl like you among them."

The guard then stomped over and grabbed her arm, moving her toward the middle of the platform, closer to the executioner.

"No!" Jiayi yelled, trying to pull from the man's grasp, but he was much stronger than she was. "No! No! I want to wake up! Why haven't I woken up?"

At the middle of the platform, the man kicked the back

of her knees, forcing her to kneel. She slammed into the wooden planks and cried out in pain.

"Please! Stop!" she cried, but the crowd continued to cheer and laugh. She raised her eyes up to the blue sky. "Zhihao! Help me!" If only he could see that she was in distress, he could shake her or remove the bracelet from her hand. Anything!

But she did not wake up. She saw the minister's arm fall, and she knew he had signaled the executioner to swing his sword.

Her eyes fell to the crowd, where she suddenly saw a familiar face. Their eyes locked.

"Wake up!" the man said.

*J*iayi gasped as she lifted her head from the table. She screamed and began to cry. She dropped the bracelet and raised her hands to her face. She could move her arms! She was back! She was alive! Still, the tears fell and she could not stop screaming.

Zhihao leaped to his feet and ran to her side, taking her in his arms.

"Jiayi!" he said, giving her a light shake. "What happened? What's wrong?"

"They...they killed me!" she said. "I...oh, the pain!" She grabbed her neck, making sure it was still attached to her body. It was, but it brought her little comfort. The other pains remained. The pain in her arms, her back, her face, her feet, and between her legs.

"No, Jiayi," Zhihao said, trying to talk in a calming voice. "You are not dead. You are alive. Everything is okay."

"No, no, no," Jiayi said as she continued to cry, rocking herself back and forth. "I killed her. It was my fault!"

"Who did you kill?" Zhihao asked.

"The maid!" Jiayi said. "Song Jier. The empress found out about the bracelet. She had me...the maid put to death. It was my fault. My fault."

Zhihao cursed in a low voice and held Jiayi tight. "You saw it?" he asked after a moment. "You saw them put her to death."

She shook her head. "No. I *was* put to death. I was her. They dragged me to the platform. The executioner raised his sword." She nearly choked on her words as she tried to tell Zhihao what happened.

"Shh," he said, patting her hair, her cheeks, her shoulders. "You don't have to say anymore. It must have been terrible. But you are safe now. You woke up in time."

Jiayi turned to him. "No! I didn't. I couldn't. I tried, but nothing happened. I called for you, but you couldn't hear me."

"I'm so sorry," Zhihao said, and she could see the pain in his eyes.

"It's not your fault," she said. "But I saw him. He was there. He told me to wake up."

"Who?" Zhihao asked.

"Eunuch Lo," Jiayi said.

TEN

Zhihao held Jiayi in his arms, feeling her body tremble, her tears soaking through his shirt. He pulled her into his chest, wishing he could do more to comfort her. But even this was dangerous. If someone saw them embracing, they could infer that something else was going on and report them to the empress. But he did not want to let her go. Not yet.

"Did you say Eunuch Lo?" Zhihao asked. She had to be mistaken.

"He was in the crowd," Jiayi said, pulling away a little bit and wiping her eyes. She seemed to be calming down. "He looked up at me and told me to wake up just as the minister signaled...signaled..."

"You don't have to say it," he said. She nodded as she pulled from his arms and sat up. "It was just a terrible dream. I know your visions are vivid, and they seem real to you in the moment, but in the end, they are just dreams."

"Are they?" Jiayi asked. "Everything I ever saw before was real. If they weren't, how would we have ever found anything? If I saw the maid executed, it must have happened. And it was all my fault!"

Zhihao wasn't sure what else to say. She had a point. Her visions had always been accurate representations of the past before. But she had never influenced someone so strongly before either. Unless she didn't.

"Jiayi," he said, "you don't know that you influenced the maid to steal the bracelet."

"Yes, I do!" she said. "I could feel her trying to stop me. I heard her voice. She said there was danger."

"I am sure she had doubts about stealing," he said. "But in the end, you don't know that you stole the bracelet. She might have done it even if you hadn't been there. After you left her, she didn't return it. She kept it. She was probably executed anyway. You just happened to have a vision at a very perilous time."

Jiayi sighed and leaned on the table as though she was exhausted. "It was terrifying," she said. "That poor girl. I don't think I can ever forgive myself."

"I understand," Zhihao said before he could stop himself.

"What?" she asked. "How can you?"

He hesitated. He didn't want to think about Eli right now. He knew that Rebecca's letter must be the reason the memory was pushing to the surface now. But he knew some of what Jiayi was feeling. For years he blamed himself for Eli's death. He still did. But Jiayi looked up at him expectantly, her eyes still shining with unshed tears.

"My friend, Eli," Zhihao said. "He died because of me."

"Oh," Jiayi said. "I remember. When I had a vision of you and Rebecca. She said you never forgave yourself for Eli's death."

Zhihao nodded. "She was right. My guilt drove us apart."

"Why?" Jiayi asked. "She lost her brother. You could have comforted each other."

Zhihao shook his head in shame. "I should have been there for her as she tried to be there for me," he said. "But, I had been thinking of her when the accident...I was supposed to be watching the workers install new support beams. I was looking at some images I thought Rebecca would find interesting. I didn't hear the workers call out. I didn't help them until it was too late."

"It was an accident," Jiayi said. "She never blamed you."

"But every time I looked at her," he said, "I was reminded of how I wasn't paying attention. He died because of me."

Jiayi rubbed her thumb over Zhihao's knuckles, back and forth. The motion and repetition were soothing.

"I'm sorry," she said. "I had no idea you carried such pain in you."

"I didn't tell you so that you would feel sorry for me," he said. "I wanted you to know that the pain, the guilt, it gets better."

"It goes away?" she asked.

"I wish I could lie to you," he said. "It never goes away. But each day, the ache hurts a little less. And eventually, you just get used to the pain."

"That's a terrible way to live," Jiayi said. "I don't think I can carry this with me for the rest of my life."

Zhihao sighed and wrapped his arm around Jiayi again, pulling her into his shoulder. "I have often thought that I would do anything to get my friend back."

"Only often?" she asked. "Not all the time? Wouldn't you do whatever it took?"

"No," he said, and he moved her so that he could look down into her eyes. "I would never risk losing you too."

Her eyes looked misty again, but for a different reason this time. He leaned down and closed his eyes as he placed his lips on hers. He thought he felt her hesitate a bit, as though she considered pulling away. But before he could stop, she leaned into him and reached up to stroke his face. He pulled her tightly to him and parted her mouth with his, she following his movements fluidly. She felt warm and soft in his arms, and her kisses were gentle, yet betrayed a hunger. Had she been hiding her feelings the same way he had been?

"Jiayi," he whispered, and she gasped and pulled away. Her eyes flew to the door, and they both saw a nosy eunuch walk by at a distance, watching them.

Jiayi climbed to her feet, but then she winced and swayed slightly. Zhihao jumped up to help her.

"Are you injured?" he asked.

"No," she said. "Just a memory of the pain."

"It will pass," he said. "I am sure of it."

"I must go," she said, but she stopped when her eyes fell on the silver bracelet still sitting on the table where she had dropped it. "Get rid of it," she whispered.

"I will," he said. She then walked out of the building, down a garden path, and out of sight.

Zhihao sighed and rubbed his hand over his head. What had he just done? What had they done? She had kissed him back, right? Of course she had. He could tell when a woman wanted him. But she had not expressed a desire to be with him through her words as he had. He didn't know if she wanted to marry him or not—not that he had actually asked her. After all, it didn't matter how much either of them wanted to marry, the empress still stood in their way.

He groaned to himself. The empress would surely find out what happened. Nothing escaped her spies in the Inner Court. Eunuchs could never be trusted. They would share any secret for the promise of a little coin.

Zhihao paced the room. He had a feeling he should leave. He did not want to be here when the empress heard he had been kissing her maid or think about which appendage she would have dispatched from his body in her fury. And yet, he didn't want to leave Jiayi to face the woman's wrath alone. The empress already had no qualms about beating her for the most contrived of slights. No wonder Jiayi took out her frustration by stealing from Empress Wu. She thought Empress Wu couldn't hurt her when they were separated by a thousand years. But Jiayi had been wrong. So very wrong. What would have happened if Jiayi hadn't woken up before the executioner's blade fell on the maid's neck? Could Jiayi have died? He feared it was possible. She had been affected by her hosts' lives before. She could learn their languages and skills. Could she also carry their pain and injuries? He didn't want to know the answer.

He had fantasized about Jiayi being able to change the past. Of her maybe using her powers to save Eli. But now, he would never ask such a thing of her. He almost didn't survive the cave-in himself. If Jiayi tried to save Eli but lost her own life in the process, that was a loss he would never be able to recover from. Even though he still carried the pain of Eli's death, he knew in his mind it had been an accident. But if Jiayi went back to try to change things and died, it would be his fault. She would be doing it for him.

He had to protect Jiayi at any cost.

He stomped across the room, pulled out a kerchief, and picked up the bracelet. It might have been a ridiculous precaution—he didn't have visions like Jiayi—but after what happened to her, he didn't want to take any chances with the thing. Why did it show Jiayi something so terrible? She thought the bracelet was calling to her. That it had a message. But what message could it be trying to send by nearly killing her? Perhaps it was a warning of some kind. Or maybe the bracelet was actually trying to hurt her. Could objects be malevolent? Could they be possessed by an entity of some sort? Who knew what the source of Jiayi's power was. He and Hu Xiaosheng had always approached her abilities as a sort of innate gift. But what they were a curse instead?

"How dare you?" a woman snapped at him as he ran into her. He had been so focused on the bracelet and Jiayi, he had not even seen...

"Der Ling!" he gasped when he saw who it was, and her mouth gaped. "I mean..." He dropped to his knee. "Princess Der Ling, forgive me. I was not watching where I was going."

"That much was obvious," she said. "Stand up." He did as she ordered, but kept his head down.

"You are the historian, Zhihao," she said.

"Yes, Your Highness," he replied. While they had seen each other many times, they had never spoken before.

"What are you doing in the Inner Court?" she asked.

"The empress allows me to visit Jiayi," he said. "To follow through on the tasks she assigns us."

"You must be quite a special man," Der Ling said, and her ladies giggled. "Do you know how many men would kill to have access to us?"

"Jiayi is the special one," he said. "I am merely her interpreter."

This seemed to catch Der Ling off guard as he saw her tilt her head from side to side as though trying to take the measure of him and come up with a reply.

"So gallant," she finally said, and she put the tip of her finger with her long ornately decorated nail guard under his chin, tilting his face up to look at her. He suddenly realized why her eyes seemed so strange to him from a distance. They were not dark brown, but a dark gray, and they reflected the light in a way he had never seen before, not even on foreigners when he was abroad.

Der Ling stuck out her lower lip in a pout. "Why should a little mouse like Jiayi have such a man as you as her defender?"

"I only have the empress to thank for that, my lady," he said. He tried to avert his gaze, but she was holding his chin up at such a sharp angle, it was hard to look anywhere else. His voice sounded strained and there was a pain when he gulped.

"What is this?" one of the ladies asked, bending down and picking up the bracelet. He had been so shocked by running into Der Ling that he did not realize it had slipped from his hand.

"Don't!" he started to say, reaching for it, but the girl held it out of his grasp from his position on his knees.

Der Ling held her hand out to the lady, and she dutifully deposited the bracelet into Der Ling's palm. Der Ling removed her finger from under Zhihao's chin, giving his neck some much-needed relief, and turned the bracelet side to side.

"Filthy," Der Ling said of the black tarnish.

"Indeed," he said. "It is quite old."

"How old?" Der Ling asked.

He suddenly realized that if Der Ling thought it was a Tang Dynasty item, she would give it to the empress, and the empress would make Jiayi touch it. He could not risk Jiayi being sent back into the body of that maid again.

"Umm...Ming," he stammered. "Ming Dynasty."

"Oh?" Der Ling asked. "Did Jiayi confirm that."

"She did," he said quickly.

"Hmm," Der Ling mused as she continued to look the bracelet over. Zhihao wondered if Der Ling could see how badly he was sweating.

"Can I keep it?" Der Ling asked suddenly.

"What?" Zhihao barked out before he could stop himself.

"It's of no use to the empress," she said. "Since it is Ming and not Tang. And it is so dirty, it must not be worth much. But it is beautiful." She slipped her hand through it and admired it on her wrist. "It suits me, don't you think, Zhihao Shaoye?"

The other ladies tittered.

"Of course," he said as he rushed through his mind to try and come up with an excuse to get it back. He had intended on finding a way to destroy it. But one did not deny a princess any request. "But...but it is not mine to give. It belongs to the university. If I don't return with it, I could be in very great trouble."

"I'm sure the university won't miss one ugly old piece of silver," Der Ling said, leaning down and talking to him as though he were a stupid child. "Aren't you?"

Zhihao gulped again. "Of course, Your Highness."

"Oh, you truly are so kind to me!" she said as she stood back up and clapped like a gleeful little girl. "I'll never forget you, Zhihao."

At that, Der Ling and her ladies continued on their walk through the garden, leaving Zhihao wondering just what had happened.

He waited until he could no longer hear their high-pitched laughs or their pot-bottom shoes tapping on the brick walkways before standing. His knees were sore from being pressed against the hard ground for so long, and he had to rub life back into them before he tried walking again.

As he limped away, he cursed to himself. Der Ling took the blasted bracelet! Now what? How was he supposed to get it back? He couldn't just leave it here without warning Jiayi. What if Der Ling asked her to touch it to confirm what he had told her? At best, Der Ling would know he lied, and then she would want to know why. At worst, she could endanger Jiayi's life if she ended up back in the body of the maid.

He paced in circles, trying to figure out what to do. If he wanted to see Jiayi, he would have to go back to the audience hall and have a eunuch summon her. But he could think of no other options.

He walked back toward the audience hall, grateful for the circulation to be returning to his knees. He was nearly there when he heard a loud gong echo over the garden. He looked up and realized the sun was setting. A eunuch quickly approached him.

"Sir, you must leave at once," the eunuch said.

"I cannot," Zhihao said. "I must see Jiayi immediately." He moved toward the audience hall, but the eunuch blocked him.

"You know the rules, sir," he said. "No man save the emperor is allowed in the Inner Court after sunset."

"It will only take a moment and is of the utmost—"

"You will be arrested, sir," the eunuch said, nodding

toward two guards who were standing at a nearby gate.

Zhihao cursed to himself again. He knew there was no way around the rule. It was a way of protecting any woman in the emperor's harem from falling pregnant by anyone other than himself. Not that the emperor had ever gotten anyone pregnant either.

"Can I send a note?" Zhihao asked. "If I write a note, will you deliver it to Jiayi for me."

"I could get in great trouble, sir," the eunuch said, which was his way of saying yes, for a price.

Zhihao reached into his sleeve and pulled out a notebook and pen. He started to write in Chinese, but when he realized that Jiayi couldn't read it, he switched to English. He didn't know if she could read English, but since she had picked up Rebecca's ability to speak English, he hoped he had picked up her ability to read as well.

Der Ling has the bracelet was all he wrote. He then folded it in half and handed it to the eunuch. He then fished some coins out of his pocket and handed those over as well. The eunuch took the coins and the paper, but cocked his head to the side like a curious bird. Zhihao grunted and then handed the eunuch two more coins.

"Make sure that Jiayi—and only Jiayi—receives this immediately," Zhihao said with as much force as he could muster.

"Of course, noble sir," the eunuch said with an exaggerated bow.

Zhihao shook his head in annoyance and walked toward the guards, who made sure to escort him all the way out of the gate. As he rode home in a rickshaw, he could not help but feel anxious. He would have to come back and warn Jiayi about the bracelet and Der Ling first thing in the morning.

ELEVEN

*J*iayi locked the door to her room and pulled the cloth across the window. Even though the empress could send for her at any moment, it was the only amount of privacy she could get.

She sat cross-legged on her bed with her back against the wall. Her sleeves were pulled over her hands, but in one hand, she held the necklace she used to visit Prince Junjie. In the other, she held the pocket watch she stole from Zhihao back when they first met.

She had never touched the pocket watch and had no idea what memories it could hold. She took it because she could, not because she needed to. She had a feeling that if Zhihao ever knew, he would be furious with her.

But maybe not.

The kiss had shocked her. It was not unpleasant—or unwelcome—but she had no idea that Zhihao had any loving feelings for her at all. She thought he only worked with her because he had to. Because the empress ordered it and because she was useful to him. She liked to think they were friendly, if not actually friends, because it made dealing with him easier. But she did not doubt that if the day came that he would need to cut her out of his life, he would.

How could she have so completely misjudged his character? He wanted to marry her. He wanted to rescue her from the empress. He had no plan for either of those things, but he was searching for answers.

But what if he found a way to marry her? What if he asked the empress for permission and the empress said yes? Would she be happy about it? She didn't know. She had never given the idea much thought. But that kiss...There was heat there. His touch ignited feelings in her she had never had when she was awake before.

Her hand clenched tightly around the gold necklace of Lady Meirong. There was only one man Jiayi had ever loved—and that was Prince Junjie. He had been the only thing that kept her going during the most difficult times. The years when she was utterly alone. He had been her comfort, her passion, her reason for living. If she could fall through time and stay with Prince Junjie forever, she would. She wanted nothing more than to save his life. In a strange way, kissing Zhihao had felt like she was being unfaithful to Prince Junjie.

But Prince Junjie didn't know her.

Jiayi didn't exist for him. Only Lady Meirong. Jiayi wiped a tear from her eye at the realization and placed the necklace aside.

She pulled up her sleeve and her hand hovered over Zhihao's pocket watch. She knew what he said, that he would never want to risk losing her to save his friend Eli. But Jiayi knew how devastating his death had been. The guilt over the execution of the maid was tearing her apart. If she could help Eli, alleviate that sense of guilt for Zhihao, she would.

"Take me to Egypt," she whispered as she closed her eyes. She could end up any time in Zhihao's past when he had the watch. But there was only one time and place she wanted to go. "Take me to Egypt." She lowered her hand and touched the watch.

*T*he sun beat down on her and the wind peppered her face with sand. She licked her lips and tasted the salt from her sweat that had slid down from her forehead. She exhaled and removed her sunglasses, running her hands over her hair and pulling the few blonde curls that had escaped back into their tie.

Blonde curls?

Jiayi looked up and saw a massive pyramid towering over her. Her jaw dropped as she craned her neck to look up the side of it.

"Never gets old, does it?" a man said as he approached.

Jiayi did not know who he was, but she felt a warm affection for him in the woman she had possessed.

"Sorry it took me so long to get here," she said. "It took forever to find a maid willing to undertake the journey from England."

"And where is she now?" he asked.

"Hiding from the sun at the hotel," she said. "I'll be surprised if she lasts the week."

"We better get to work then," he said. "Just in case you end up summoned back home for the terrible crime of traveling unescorted."

"I won't tell Mother if you don't," she said. She paused

for a moment before she tried and failed to slyly ask, "And where is Theodore?"

Jiayi felt her heart skip at the mention of Zhihao's English name. She had to be Rebecca. She wondered if this man she was speaking to was Rebecca's brother, Eli. The friend Zhihao wanted to save.

"He's around here somewhere," Eli said. "The workers need to bring in some more beams to support the lower level."

Jiayi remembered Zhihao saying something about beams and how he wasn't paying attention when the accident occurred. If she wanted to save Eli, she was sure she needed to do something now, but what?

"Why don't you wait here for him?" Eli said, wiggling his eyebrows suggestively, and Rebecca scoffed. "I'm going in. I want to take a few more notes before it gets too late."

"Fine—" Rebecca started to say, but Jiayi cut her off. "No! Stay here...with me."

"Don't worry, old gal," Eli said. "He's just as anxious to see you." He then gave her a smile and turned to go through the small opening of the pyramid before she could object further.

Jiayi ran her hands through her hair and paced before the opening to the pyramid. Should she go down there? Drag him out? Tell someone that it wasn't safe?

"Rebecca!" Zhihao called out, and Jiayi turned toward him, her mouth curving into a smile despite the situation. He nearly jogged over to her and took her hand, bringing it to his mouth. "How I missed you."

Jiayi was shocked at how different he looked. Younger. Happier. A man in love. A man without the years of guilt weighing on his soul.

"I missed you too," Rebecca said, then Jiayi interjected. "Zhihao, I need to tell you—"

"Zhihao?" he said with a laugh. "Since when do you call me that?"

If Jiayi could blush, she would have. She needed to be more careful if she was going to try to control the people she inhabited.

"I mean, Theodore," Jiayi said with a chuckle. "I need to talk to you about something."

"And I you," Zhihao said, cupping her cheek. "But not here. Too many people and this weather is oppressive. Tonight, back at the hotel, okay?"

"It's important," Jiayi said.

"*Efendim!*" a man called out. He was carrying a load of timbers over his shoulder.

"Right!" Zhihao called with a wave. He pulled out his pocket watch to check the time. The same one Jiayi was holding now. "Let me just deal with this, then we can go back and celebrate your arrival."

He didn't wait for an answer as he waved to the worker and then went into the pyramid the same way that Eli had gone.

Jiayi cursed to herself as she tried to figure out what to do. She didn't want to risk hurting herself—or Rebecca—by going into the pyramid. But that was where the accident would be. She was able to come to the right time and place, but she might never come back here again. She needed to do something now if she wanted to have any chance of saving Eli.

She walked over to the pyramid entrance, but it was blocked with men trying to get the beams inside. Zhi— Theodore!" she called out, hoping he could hear her. "Eli!

Answer me! I need you!" But no one responded. She had no idea how deep into the pyramid they were.

She followed the last worker into the tunnel. But when she was only a few steps in, she heard shouting and the ground started to shake. Suddenly, she was pushed against the wall as the workers shoved past her trying to get out of the narrow tunnel. She was too late! She tried to move with the men to go back out herself, but the men took no note of her as they clamored over one another in a panic. Someone stomped her foot and elbowed her in the chest, knocking the wind out of her.

"Zhihao!" she screamed as the rumbling intensified and the sand fell thicker onto her face and into her eyes.

She felt a hand on her arm drag her along with the tidal wave of escapees toward the opening. As she stepped into the sun, she turned back to look at the tunnel and heard what sounded like an explosion, followed by a plume of dust as the inside of the pyramid collapsed.

She looked at whoever had helped her and saw Zhihao. Their eyes met.

"Eli?" she asked, and Zhihao's face crumpled in pain. She pulled him into her arms as he fell to the ground, releasing the most terrible cry of pain she had ever heard from a man.

Jiayi gasped as she woke up. Her chest was in pain and she had fallen to her side. She coughed and sputtered and had difficulty getting her lungs to fill. How long had she been gone? Usually, when her real body ran out of air, she woke automatically. But this time, as she gasped over and over, she felt as though she had been drowning. She had already nearly died in a vision once today, and now she was having problems breathing. She was supposed to be growing stronger in her powers, but she felt as though she was losing control. As if the visions were becoming more dangerous.

And despite the risk she took, she had still failed!

Jiayi tossed the watch onto the bed and buried her face in her hands. What was the point of being able to travel back in time if she couldn't help those she loved? She'd done nothing to save Prince Junjie's life either so far. She didn't even know how or why he died. She felt so useless.

She stood and opened the window covering and was shocked when she saw it was completely dark out. It had only been sunset when she closed the door. She had been unconscious for much longer than she thought. She did need to be more careful. It would be devastating if she went to sleep and never woke back up.

"*T*his makeup pot was sent as a gift from the Minister of Finance," the empress said as she held it up to Jiayi. "He vowed that it once belonged to Empress Wu."

Jiayi did not know much about archeology, but she had picked up enough to know whether something was old or not. After all, Empress Wu had just thrown a dozen makeup pots at her recently. This didn't look like any of those.

"Where did he get it?" Jiayi dared to ask.

"He said it belonged to his wife," the empress said. "A wedding gift from her great-grandparents."

Jiayi nodded. She imagined the grandparents must not

have been very fond of their granddaughter to have spent so little on a wedding gift.

"The ministers seemed to have heard of my desire to find anything belonging to Empress Wu," the empress said. "They have been sending me whole boxes of items." She motioned to a large chest full of cups, makeup pots, chopsticks, and jewelry—none of which looked to be from the Tang era to Jiayi.

"That is very generous of them," Jiayi said.

"Generosity has nothing to do with it," the empress sneered. "They are only hoping I will heap praise upon them for pleasing me so. Still, if the item we are looking for is among this rubbish, it could be worth it."

"Indeed, Your Majesty," Jiayi said. "Have you sent for Zhihao? He could probably tell you which items would be authentically Tang and the best to start with."

The empress scoffed and waved her hand. "He's busy," she whined. "Can you believe that? Called before the university overseer. He cannot come until this afternoon."

"But it could be worth the wait," one of the empress's maids said. "If what you need is here, Prince Kang could be the next emperor!"

Several of the other ladies simpered behind their sleeves. Der Ling just rolled her eyes.

"Shut up, stupid girl," the empress snapped, and all the girls went silent. "We are not going to wait for Zhihao. Jiayi will test the items now. Zhihao should know better than to try my patience."

Jiayi stammered. "But...but, Your Majesty, there are so many things. It could be a terrible waste of your time—"

"Get to work!" the empress ordered as she grabbed Jiayi's hand and thrust the makeup pot she had been holding into it.

Jiayi cried out and then fell away.

When she woke up, she had to rub her head where she hit it as she fell to the ground.

"Well?" the empress asked, standing over her.

Jiayi groaned as she pushed herself to her knees. "I...I was a noblewoman, but not from the Tang Dynasty. Her clothing suggested she was a lady from not very long ago."

"Humph!" the empress said, smashing the makeup pot to the ground. "Bring me that goblet," she said to the maids, pointing to the chest.

"Your Majesty," Jiayi said, kneeling with her forehead to the floor, "I am sorry, but I must rest. I won't be able to have another vision."

"I am tired of waiting!" the empress said. She took the goblet that the maid offered her and she reached for Jiayi's hand. Jiayi did not fight her because she did not expect to be able to have another vision again so soon. But in a moment, she was in a new place, in the body of another woman. An elderly woman at a wedding. This time, she was in the Ming era.

Wake up, wake up, wake up, she chanted to herself. She did not want to stay under any longer than necessary. The idea of being stuck in some random time in history was terrifying.

She gasped as she awoke again, apparently by running out of breath. This gave her some small comfort.

"It worked!" the empress cheered. "What did you see?"

Jiayi tried to push herself to kneeling, but her head was swimming and she was exhausted. She barely had the strength to move.

"An old woman," she said. "A wedding. Not the empress."

"Bring me another!" the empress said.

"No," Jiayi mumbled. "Please."

"No?" the empress asked. She grabbed Jiayi by the arm and shook her. "You will do as you are ordered!"

"Of course!" Jiayi said. "I'm sorry."

A pearl necklace, an embroidered shoe, and another item Jiayi couldn't identify because she could barely see straight were all thrust at her in quick succession.

"Please!" Jiayi cried. "Stop!"

"Wait," Der Ling finally said just as the empress was about to give Jiayi a piece of jade. "I have something."

"What is it?" the empress asked.

Der Ling reached into her pocket and pulled out a silver bracelet.

Jiayi would have screamed in fear if she had the strength when she realized it was the same silver bracelet that had nearly killed her the day before. She had told Zhihao to get rid of it. How did Der Ling find it? Had she been watching them when Jiayi touched it? Did she see them kiss? Why would she want to hurt her?

The empress and Der Ling had some words back and forth, but Jiayi could barely make them out. She only wanted to sleep.

"Fine," the empress finally said, and Der Ling stepped toward Jiayi. Two maids helped Jiayi sit up, and she did not have the strength to fight them.

"Why?" Jiayi asked as Der Ling crouched before her.

A cruel smile spread across Der Ling's face as she picked up Jiayi's hand. She pulled a piece of paper out of the fold in her robe at her chest. Jiayi's eyes could not read the words very well, but she could see Der Ling's name.

"If you and Zhihao try to go behind my back again, I'll make sure you regret it," Der Ling said. She then thrust the bracelet into Jiayi's hand with as much force as if it had been a dagger to the chest.

Nothing happened.

Jiayi sighed in relief. Finally, her powers were spent—at least for the moment. Or perhaps the bracelet had nothing else to show her. Either way, she was more than grateful to be spared another vision. She couldn't help but smile a little, which Der Ling seemed to take as a personal insult. She slapped Jiayi across the face.

"She's useless!" Der Ling said.

The empress grunted her dissatisfaction. "Take her away," she said, and Jiayi felt the hands of two of the eunuchs lifting her up. She had no idea if they were taking her to her room, the dungeon, or throwing her out on the street.

She didn't really care.

TWELVE

Zhihao woke with a gasp, sweating and breathing hard. He looked to the window and saw that the sky was just starting to lighten. He was surprised he was able to sleep at all, he was so worried about Jiayi. If Der Ling had her touch the bracelet...

He tossed the cover aside and tried to stand. He needed to go to the palace immediately and try to gain access, but he was so dizzy he nearly collapsed. He sat back down on the bed and rubbed his head.

He then started to remember bits and pieces from his dream. There was a large gathering of people, like an important social event. But there were men and women present, so it was not very realistic, or from the current time period. Maybe all this talk about the Tang Dynasty had influenced his dreams. Now that he thought more about it, the clothing and hairstyles were distinctly Tang.

He had been walking through the crowd of people. Men tried to talk to him and women wanted to dance, but he ignored them all. He was looking for someone in particular.

Finally, the crowd parted and he saw her. The most

beautiful woman at the gathering. She looked at him and smiled.

Jiayi.

He felt his heart glow and something like sparks flow through his body all the way to his fingertips. But Jiayi gave him only a polite bow before turning back to her companion. Zhihao recognized him from Jiayi's drawings. Prince Junjie. One of the most handsome men in history. And Jiayi stared up at the man with utter rapture. Junjie reached out and lightly touched her cheek, and her skin blazed with pink.

"Jiayi!" Zhihao had called out.

She looked back at him in shock, followed by fear.

Then he had woken up.

He picked up a cold cup of tea from beside his bed. "Ayi!" he called for the maid, who appeared only a moment later. He told her to bring him fresh tea. She bobbed a curtsey and rushed away.

Zhihao rubbed his head and then took a deep breath before standing again. This time, he was able to stay on his feet.

He poured himself a bowl of wash water for his hands, face, and arms. The maid brought the tea, which he drank eagerly.

"Go out to the street and hire the first rickshaw puller you can find," he told the maid.

He dressed quickly and was practically running out the door when one of the family's older male servants approached him.

"A summons for you, young master," the man said.

"It can wait," Zhihao said.

"From the university chancellor," the man continued. "He demands to see you presently."

Zhihao ripped the paper out of the man's hand and glanced at it. It did seem to be urgent. The note said that all faculty were to be present or could risk termination.

Zhihao cursed to himself. He could not risk angering the chancellor. He had already been absent so often on business for the empress. He crumpled the summons up and stormed out the door to the rickshaw the maid had found for him. As he climbed up, though, she tried to stop him.

"Summons for you, sir," she said.

"Another one?" he asked, exasperated. The maid only shrugged. "Tell whoever it is that I have urgent business elsewhere and will respond when I can." He then sat down and told the driver to get him to the university as quickly as possible.

*A*fter Zhihao's urgent meeting with the university chancellor—not that Zhihao considered meeting next year's fellows urgent—he rushed to the Forbidden City to check on Jiayi. But he was stopped at the gate and prevented from entering the palace at all.

"The empress herself has given permission for me to call on Jiayi whenever I deem it prudent!" Zhihao argued with the guard.

"Jiayi is unavailable at the moment," the guard replied, making Zhihao sick to his stomach. Was he too late? Had something happened to her?

"Where is she?" he asked, trying to remain calm but certain his face betrayed his concern.

"The empress said you may enter the palace only when she summons you," the guard said with a bit of a smirk. He seemed to enjoy using his power to cause Zhihao distress.

"I just need to know if Jiayi is safe," Zhihao said. "Is she unharmed?"

"We don't share palace business with outsiders," another guard said, shoving Zhihao in the shoulder and slamming the western gate shut.

Zhihao banged on the hard wood. "Open at once!" he demanded, but he could hear the guards laughing at him from the other side. He walked along the wall, trying to find a way inside. But, of course, the Forbidden City was secure.

He was not sure what to do. He did not want to just abandon Jiayi, but what could he do? He could not get inside. And even if he did, he would not know where to find her. And if he were caught inside, in direct opposition to the empress's orders, he shuddered to imagine what the punishment would be.

After a few more minutes of pacing, he had to accept that there was nothing he could do. The only way he could get inside to see Jiayi would be with the empress's permission. He would have to wait.

He sighed and put his hands in his pockets as he decided to return home even though he should have gone back to the university. Hu Xiaosheng would wonder where he was. But he had a feeling that the meeting that morning had cost him his chance to see Jiayi. He was also avoiding Lian. Lian had tried to stop him after the meeting, no doubt to ask him about meeting Jiayi, but he had ignored him and rushed out as quickly as possible.

As he walked past the kitchen, he saw his mother standing over the fire of the stove, about to toss a piece of paper into it.

"What is that?" Zhihao asked.

"Never you mind," she said, releasing the paper and sending it up in smoke. He grimaced. He knew it was another letter from Rebecca. He shouldn't care. He had just declared his feelings for Jiayi. Well, almost. He didn't tell her he was in love with her, only that he would marry her if he could. And she had not said anything to indicate she had feelings for him at all. But...that kiss...

"There is something here for you," his mother said, walking over and pulling another envelope out of her pocket. As she handed it to him, his heart turned to stone when he saw it was a summons from the empress. He groaned and laid his head against the doorframe. This must have been the summons the maid received just after the one he had gotten from the university.

"Did you send a reply?" he asked.

"I did not think it wise to ignore the empress," his mother said. "We told her you were urgently needed at the university but that you would call on her as soon as you were available."

"I did go there after the meeting," Zhihao said. "But she would not admit me. Said she would send for me if I were needed again."

His mother grimaced and then shook her head. She walked down the hall to one of the sitting rooms and took a seat. It was hard for her to stand for very long with her bound feet. She told a maid who was in the room cleaning the floor to bring them some tea.

"The empress is a temperamental woman," his mother said as she took her seat.

"That is an understatement," Zhihao said, sitting nearby.

"How is the girl?" his mother asked. "Jiayi?"

"I saw her yesterday, and she was well," he said. "But...I have a feeling...I don't know. I wanted to see her today."

"Do you have reason to worry about her?" his mother asked.

"Possibly," he said, crossing his legs and fidgeting with his shoe. "Or I could be overreacting. I don't know."

"It can be difficult when you care for someone but cannot see them often," his mother said knowingly.

Zhihao stopped messing with his shoe and looked at her. "What?" he asked.

His mother sighed. "Love is a stupid reason to marry. It is dangerous. When love fades, it can put whole families at risk. And yet, I know there is something special about that girl. I think even I could love her like a daughter very easily."

"Ma," Zhihao groaned. "What are you talking about? We've been through this. I can't marry Jiayi."

"Have you asked the empress?" She looked at him like the stupid boy he knew he sometimes was.

"No," Zhihao said. "She is allowing Jiayi to work with me. If she thought I wanted to marry Jiayi, she might think I have already been improper with her. What if she not only refuses the marriage but prevents me from seeing her even for work?"

"Then we can make arrangements for a real marriage," his mother said. "It is time."

"I don't want to think about this right now," Zhihao said. "I have enough on my mind."

"If you were a filial son, a marriage would be first in your mind!" his mother snapped.

"I have done everything to be a good son," Zhihao said. "I came home. I work hard."

"It is not even noon meal," she said. "Why are you here and not at work?"

Zhihao rubbed his face and then stood. "Fine! I'll leave."

"No!" his mother said. "Sit down. I will compose a letter to the empress requesting permission for you to marry Jiayi."

"I don't want to risk not seeing her again," Zhihao said. "This is important."

"We need to consider what sort of assets we could bring to such a marriage," his mother said, ignoring him. He knew there was no sense in arguing. If his mother was intent on this course of action, there was nothing he could do to stop her.

"I can't think of any," Zhihao said. "We are not high-ranking enough to marry a palace maid. We aren't even Manchu."

His mother nodded slowly. "This is true. We are not high-ranking in the world of the Machu. But in the world of the Han, we were once royalty."

"What are you talking about?" Zhihao asked with an exasperated sigh.

"Why do you think you were among the young men selected by Prince Gong to study abroad?" she asked.

"Because I was smart?" he said.

"Yes," his mother said as she stood and went to a bookshelf across the room. She poked and prodded at a few things, looking for something. "But you were also from a good lineage. Someone the Manchu nobles might accept as a young minister upon your return. Of course, that never happened."

The Manchu nobles would not accept a Han of any lineage among their ranks, much less a bunch of young men who had been instilled with Western ideals.

"During the Ming Dynasty, we had an ancestor who was a nobleman, I think I remember Father saying," Zhihao said, standing and walking over to the shelf, wondering what his mother was looking for. "But none of that mattered after the Qing came to power."

"It wasn't the Ming," his mother said. "It was the Tang."

Zhihao blinked and stared at her for a moment. "The Tang? Are you sure?"

"Ah!" she said, finding what she was looking for. She pulled a box down and handed it to Zhihao.

He held it carefully, as though the answers to all his problems were inside this box.

"*Aiyo*," his mother said, taking it from him and opening it. Inside were two golden bracelets, one engraved with a phoenix, the other with a dragon. They were quite heavy, and the style and markings on the inside indicated that they were indeed from the Tang era.

"What are these?" Zhihao asked.

"During the time of Empress Wu, one of your father's ancestors was a powerful warlord," his mother said. "In order to submit to the empress's rule, he was allowed to marry into the royal family. A girl named Meirong. These bracelets were among the wedding gifts the warlord gave to her."

"So, you are saying that Father's family was descended from Empress Wu?" he asked. "I'm descended from the empress?"

HIs mother beamed. "You always were my little prince."

There was something significant here he was missing. It could not be a coincidence that he was holding Tang era gold—gold used in a marriage arrangement with a member of Empress Wu's family—in his hand at just the time that the empress had ordered him to find items that would allow

Jiayi to contact Empress Wu. But he needed to find out what that connection was.

"Why are you sharing this with me now?" Zhihao asked.

"Because," his mother said, "if the empress knows you are descended from a great empress, it might be enough status to allow you to marry Jiayi."

His mother had no idea how right she was. He had a feeling that if Jiayi touched the bracelets, she might just find a way to allow the empress to rule in her own right. Maybe then, the empress would be so grateful that she would allow him to marry Jiayi in thanks.

"Wait," Zhihao said. "I need to find a way to talk to Jiayi first." He couldn't tell his mother about Jiayi's powers, but he did not want Jiayi to touch the bracelets and they turn out to be useless in front of the empress. He needed Jiayi to touch them privately first. Then, if they were what the empress was looking for, he could present them to the empress and then ask for a marriage while the empress was sure to be pleased with him.

"You said the empress would not let you see her," his mother said.

"Exactly," he said. "If the empress is displeased with me, she will not consent to a marriage no matter how high we rank. I need to find a way back into her good graces first."

"What are you going to do?" his mother asked.

"Jiayi isn't the only person in the Forbidden City I know," Zhihao said.

THIRTEEN

"Are you all right?"

Jiayi had to struggle to open her eyes. But when she did so, she was greeted by the worried face of Prince Junjie.

"I...I don't know," Jiayi said. "What happened?"

"I was hoping you could tell me," Junjie said with a chuckle as he helped her sit. She winced and her hand went to her head. "I found you passed out on the floor, so I brought you here."

Jiayi looked around and saw that she was in one of the sitting rooms of Prince Junjie's private house inside the palace of Chang'an. A place she knew well as Lady Meirong. Her hand flew to her neck, but she wasn't wearing the wedding necklace she usually was when she visited the prince. This must be another dream.

"I don't remember," she finally said. Even in a dream, she didn't think she could tell Junjie that the empress had forced her to travel through time so many times she fell unconscious.

"I should send for a doctor," Junjie said, but as he moved to leave, Jiayi grabbed the sleeve of his coat.

"No," she said, and he sat back beside her. "I will be fine. I just need to sit for a moment."

The prince put his arm around her shoulder. "Stay as long as you like."

Jiayi settled against him. He felt firm and warm. Exactly as he did when she was in a vision. When she slept at night, she dreamed. That was how she knew the visions she had during the day were something different. Night dreams were vague, intangible, like a thin mist in the early dawn. But this did not feel like a dream. It was as real as a vision. But how was that possible if she wasn't touching an item?

"Will Lady Meirong be angry if she catches you with me?" Jiayi asked.

"What do you know of Lady Meirong and me?" Junjie asked, surprised.

Jiayi laughed. "Everyone knows."

"Oh dear," he said. "I suppose we have not been as discreet as we thought."

"Not at all," Jiayi said, and Junjie laughed with her.

"It doesn't matter," he said. "I am sure you know that we cannot marry. I have heard that there is a warlord who has asked the empress for a royal bride as part of an alliance negotiation. I believe he has his eye on Meirong."

"I am sorry," Jiayi said. "It must be difficult to see the person you love married to someone else."

"We will see what happens," he said, pulling Jiayi to him more tightly. Jiayi heard him sigh and thought his mind was suddenly elsewhere.

"What is wrong?" Jiayi asked.

"I am taking care of you," Junjie said. "I will not burden with you with the troubles of court life."

"Please, tell me," Jiayi said. "Maybe I can help you."

The prince hesitated, but his concerns must have been great indeed. "For the first time in my life, I am afraid."

"Of what?" Jiayi asked. Junjie was a warrior. A relative of the empress. What could he possibly have to fear?

"My enemies are conspiring against me," he said. "But this is not a battle on a field where I can see the blows coming and defend myself. I have been a fool to discount the threats here at court for so long. I do not have the insight to know who I can trust."

"Maybe I can help you," Jiayi said.

"You?" Junjie asked, looking at her with laughter in his eyes. He moved a strand of hair behind her ear. "What can you do for me?"

"I'm nobody," she said. "Who would look twice at a maid?"

"I did," he said.

"Few others could say the same," Jiayi said. "You are a man of uncommon kindness."

The prince kissed her forehead and hugged her tight. "Oh, Jiayi. This world is too dark for the likes of us."

"Maybe we can save each other," she said.

*J*iayi groaned as a pounding on the door woke her, forcing her from her beautiful dream. Her head throbbed and the light stung as she tried to open her eyes. As she slowly came to, she realized that she was freezing and her arm was asleep. Her arm was hanging off the bed and she was not covered with a blanket. The fire in her small fireplace had long burned out. It seemed that the eunuchs had tossed her onto her bed unceremoniously, without taking care that she would be comfortable or not die of a chill.

"Jiayi!" she heard Prince Kang call as he banged on her door again.

"Y-y-yes!" she finally stuttered. What had happened? She had just been with Prince Junjie. Was it a dream? Did it have something to do with all the items the empress had made her touch? What was Prince Kang doing here? She forced herself to sit up and made sure she was decently covered. She walked over to the door and lifted the latch. The prince nearly burst into the room at the sound of the click.

"Jiayi!" he said with relief when he saw here. "Damn, it's cold in here."

It was not a cold time of year, but there was little sunlight in Jiayi's small room, so it was always cold without a fire.

The prince stuck his head back out of the room and yelled at a maid to bring firewood and hot tea.

"You don't have to do that," Jiayi said.

Prince Kang ushered her to the bed and urged her to sit down. He picked up a blanket and wrapped it around her shoulders.

"I heard what my aunt did to you," he said, sitting beside her. "I could not believe it. You are truly precious. Valuable to her. How could she do such a terrible thing?"

Jiayi started to speak, but the maid arrived with a tea tray and a basket of wood.

"Pour the tea," Kang ordered the girl. He then took the basket from her and got to work starting a fire.

"Please, that is beneath you. I can—" Jiayi tried to say, but she suddenly felt woozy again and put a hand to her head. The maid rushed over and offered her a cup of tea.

Jiayi nodded her thanks and drank the tea eagerly. The tea was red, which would help her feel better.

In a moment, the prince had the fire going and Jiayi had drunk two cups of tea and was feeling immensely better.

The prince dismissed the maid and once again sat by Jiayi on the bed.

"Thank you," Jiayi said. "I am feeling better already."

"Can you tell me what happened?" Kang asked her.

"The empress is impatient for answers," Jiayi said. "She made me touch items over and over again. Before, it could take days for my strength to build up enough for me to have another vision after touching an item. But, lately, I have been able to have visions more often. The empress noticed. She made me have so many visions, I passed out. It was too much."

Kang stood up and paced, anger clear on his face. "I will have words with her about this."

"No!" Jiayi said. "Do not anger her. I am used to being the object of her wrath. If she turns on you, what will happen?"

"She won't hurt me," he said. "So what if she sends me back home?"

"But don't you want to be emperor?" Jiayi asked. "Think of all the good you could do."

"It would not be worth it if the cost were your life," Kang said.

"Perhaps you being emperor would be worth one life," Jiayi said.

"Not to me," Kang said. "I will not sit on a throne of blood."

Jiayi shook her head and moved to pour herself another cup of tea, but the prince stopped her, taking the cup from her and serving her himself.

"This is highly improper," Jiayi said as she accepted the cup.

"The way my aunt treats you is improper," he said, still fuming. "The empress truly believes that you are the only way I will become emperor. Yet she endangers your life!"

"I am her possession!" Jiayi said sharply, finding the strength to stand. She was feeling more angry than grateful for his concern. "She can do with me what she wills. This is how my life is. I must accept it."

"How can you just let her hurt you?" Prince Kang asked.

"What am I to do about it?" Jiayi asked. "I told you that I have no money and nowhere to go. I am not a princess or a lady. I have no family. I have no work to support myself outside the palace walls. Being dissatisfied with my life will only make living that much harder. At least I have food and protection here. Better to be abused by the empress than any man who takes a fancy to me."

The prince's face fell and the color drained away. He probably had never considered that her life would be far more dangerous on the outside. For a man of such privilege, he did not realize that a life of abuse at the empress's hands was preferred to almost any other life she could live.

"I'm sorry," the prince said, sinking into Jiayi's only chair, which let out a tired creak as he did so. He tensed and then fidgeted before trusting the old pile of wood to support his weight. Jiayi shook her head. Had he never owned a piece of squeaky furniture before?

Jiayi placed the cup back on the tea tray and folded her hands within her long sleeves. She noticed that the room had warmed considerably since the prince lit the fire.

"Thank you for your concern," she said. "And for lighting the fire."

The prince waved her thanks away. "It was the least I

could do." He rubbed his chin in thought for a moment. Jiayi slowly sank back onto the bed. It was not right for her to sit in the prince's presence, but she had to admit she was still tired from the ordeal the day before.

After a moment, the prince cleared his throat. "What do you think the empress would do if you stopped having visions for her?"

"Imprison me," Jiayi said. "Or throw me out. It would depend on how angry she was."

"But if the empress dismissed you, you would be free," the prince said.

"But then what would I do?" she asked.

"Leave this place," the prince said. "Or marry."

Her heart skipped a beat. Zhihao had said that he would marry her if he could. If the empress dismissed her, he could follow through on his promise. But Jiayi shook her head.

"I can't just tell the empress that my powers no longer work," Jiayi said. "She would force me to touch an item and I would fall into a vision. She would see that I lied."

Kang hesitated before asking, "Have you ever tried not having a vision?"

"I don't control them," Jiayi said, letting her long sleeves fall over her hands. "That is why I have to be so careful about touching anything."

"But you said you were having visions more often," Kang said. "Have your powers been growing stronger? If you can have them more often, maybe you could have them less often as well."

Jiayi's mouth gaped a bit. She had been so focused on training her powers to happen more often. To control her actions while she was in a vision. On changing the past. She had never thought about training to refuse to fall into a trance at all. How different would her life be if she could choose when to have a vision?

"I've never tried," Jiayi admitted.

"I think you should," Kang said. "This cannot continue. You need to find a way to be less useful to the empress."

"But she will be furious," Jiayi said. "She will certainly beat me. What if she—" She gasped and her hand flew to her neck at the thought of the thieving maid being executed. "What if she kills me? No! It's too risky."

The prince jumped from his seat and grabbed her forearms. "I will not let her," he said. "I will protect you."

"How?" Jiayi asked. "You are just a prince. We are all subject to her whims."

"Not if I am emperor," Kang said. "Instead of helping the empress grow more powerful, help me. Make me emperor."

"I don't know how," Jiayi said.

The prince smiled at her and tapped her nose. "I believe in you, Jiayi. You will find a way."

Jiayi shook her head. If she had not found a way to help the empress—a woman who already sat on the throne and ruled China—how would she ever be able to help Kang, a man without a proper claim to the throne?

She thought about Der Ling and Empress Wu's dagger. Maybe the answer was there. Der Ling was convinced that there was more to the dagger than met the eye. And Jiayi had to agree. There was power in that dagger. Similar to the power she had felt emanating from the silver bracelet. She shuddered. The bracelet had nearly cost her her life. The dagger could be just as dangerous. She wasn't sure if she wanted to risk touching it again. But she knew Der Ling would not give up. But maybe she could use whatever she learned from the dagger to help Kang instead of Der Ling.

But should she help Kang? She didn't know him. He was

gentle with her and spoke pretty words, but he could be trying to use her just like everyone else was. He was only using a different tactic—kindness instead of force.

"Why should I help you become emperor?" Jiayi asked.

Kang laughed. "Don't you think I would be a good emperor?"

"I don't know," Jiayi said. She licked her lips before daring to say, "Should a revolutionary rule China?"

This time, it was Kang's mouth that gaped. He took a step back and let out a short laugh. He started to say something, but then thought better of it. He looked at her, then cocked his head to the side and looked at her again.

"There is far more to you than I thought," he finally said. "And I have always thought quite highly of you."

Jiayi couldn't help but smirk at his response. He thought that she had somehow learned the truth of his past when, really, it had been Zhihao who had told her. Zhihao would be shocked when she told him he was right.

When Jiayi didn't respond, the prince asked, "Are you a revolutionary?"

Jiayi shook her head, but said nothing.

The prince laughed out loud. "You don't trust me? Even knowing that I put myself at great risk by being here at the palace?"

"Are you?" Jiayi asked. "Or are you right where you should be?"

"Ah!" the prince said. "You think I am a spy. Here to expose the revolutionaries to the empress."

Jiayi did not respond. She was not going to say anything to accidentally implicate herself or anyone else.

"That would be a smart plan," the prince said. "Too smart for most of the empress's idiot ministers." When Jiayi stayed quiet, he continued. "I am not a spy, Jiayi. And I am not a revolutionary in the sense that I want to abolish the Qing Dynasty. But I do want to make changes. The country is dying, choking under old rules and old ways of thinking. We need to modernize. Expand. Give the people more of a say. Institute a parliament. Reform taxes and land rights. Appoint more Han to higher level positions. If the throne does not change, and change quickly, it will be overthrown."

Jiayi knew nothing of a parliament or taxes, but she knew that Zhihao would. She would have to tell him what Kang had said before she could decide if she could fully trust him or not.

"I need to speak to Zhihao," she finally said. "He will know what to do."

"Good," the prince said. "Because he is anxious to see you as well."

"He is?" she asked.

"He came here to see you, but the empress forbade it," Kang explained.

"Why?" Jiayi asked.

"You know how she is," Kang said. "Lashing out at every pretend slight."

Jiayi nodded. "Then how do you know he wants to see me?"

"He wrote to me," Kang said. "Said he was worried about you but that he might have found the item the empress is looking for."

The dagger? Jiayi wanted to ask. But she didn't know if that was possible. But Der Ling did have the silver bracelet. Perhaps he traded her for it.

"But if the empress has forbidden me from seeing Zhihao, what are we to do?" Jiayi asked.

"Wait here," the prince said. "I will take care of everything."

Jiayi sighed and sat uneasily on the edge of her bed. She didn't like the idea of not being able to do anything. Of having to wait on a man she wasn't sure she could trust.

But as the prince left, he looked back at her and smiled. She couldn't help but smile back. She blushed and pushed a strand of hair behind her ear. Then the prince closed the door.

FOURTEEN

Zhihao shot off a message to Prince Kang about Jiayi. So many times, Kang had insisted that he was a friend to Zhihao. Well, this was his chance to prove it. He told Kang that the empress had forbidden him from seeing Jiayi, but that he had an item he thought might be what the empress was looking for. He didn't tell the prince what it was, but he said that it was important for Jiayi to test the item first, before telling the empress, lest she find more reasons to banish him from court.

As Zhihao waited for a response from the prince, he paced. He did not want to leave the house for fear he would miss a response from Kang. But there was little he could do at home. He had few research materials and no one to talk to aside from his mother, who was busy composing her letter of proposal for Zhihao and Jiayi. He had no hope that the empress would actually accept the arrangement. The empress wanted Jiayi under her own thumb at all times. She would not want to have to go through Jiayi's husband to have access to her and her powers. Of course, the amount of time Jiayi and Zhihao already spent together was scandalous. And Jiayi had no guardian. Any hint of impropriety in the Inner Court could taint the reputations of all of the ladies living there. Marrying Jiayi to Zhihao could preserve the sanctity of the emperor's ladies.

Or the empress might be so offended by the proposal that she could banish Zhihao from the palace and he would never see Jiayi again.

That was why he hoped to see Jiayi first, before asking for a marriage arrangement. He needed to learn the truth about the wedding bracelets his mother gave him. And he needed to know if he could trust Kang if the empress tried to keep Jiayi from him.

Finally, at the end of the day, Zhihao received a reply from Prince Kang, but there was not much too it. He said that Jiayi was safe and to wait for more information.

Still, those few words were of some comfort. His mind had been running over all sorts of terrifying possibilities. What if Jiayi was locked in a dungeon? What if the empress had beaten her unconscious? What if she was dead?

Or what if Kang was lying?

The momentary relief at receiving the note from the prince quickly gave way to a new round of anxiety. He realized that he had not heard anything from Lian. Of course, he had been avoiding him at first. He didn't want to talk any more about Jiayi with him. But after a day or two, he had stopped intentionally avoiding Lian because he simply wasn't around. He had been so caught up in everything else, he hadn't realized that Lian could be in danger. But there was nothing he could do. Other than Lian, Zhihao had no contacts among the revolutionaries in the city. He had made it a point to avoid anyone who spoke openly about their dissatisfaction with the Manchu government.

Even though he would be happy to see the Manchu fall, it was simply too dangerous to talk about such things publicly.

As the twilight of the evening turned to night, and one by one the members of Zhihao's household slipped off to bed, Zhihao was soon sitting in front of a fireplace alone and unable to sleep.

He held the golden wedding bracelets in his hands, spinning them, running his fingers over the engravings, passing them from one hand to the other. He had no idea what time it was when he finally felt his head start to droop.

"*I* am so pleased that you wish to make a marriage alliance with one of my nieces," Empress Wu said as she looked down from her throne at him.

Zhihao looked down and saw that he was dressed in the clothes of a Tang-era gentleman. He must be dreaming again.

"As are we, Your Majesty," he said with a bow. "To no longer have to defend my territory by the sword, but for my sons to inherit it is a great blessing for my family and my people."

"Then I suggest you chose a girl with ample curves suitable for bearing many children," the elderly empress said with a chuckle. Everyone else within hearing laughed as well. Zhihao smiled and gave the empress the fist in palm salute.

"I trust you have brought a suitable engagement gift with you this evening," the empress continued.

"Of course," Zhihao said, reaching into a bag tied at his waist and pulling out the two gold bracelets. "This is but a taste of the gold we will shower on the bride and her family."

"Excellent," the empress said. "Well, all of the young ladies are present this evening. Chose the one you most desire."

Zhihao bowed and backed away from the empress. He then mingled with the crowd, wondering how he would know the Lady Meirong when he saw her. There were many young ladies present, along with princes, generals, and magistrates. He had a feeling that the gathering would have been an important night of politicking for his warlord ancestor. He wondered if he would be as savvy in his dream version.

After a moment of watching the many women talking, laughing, and dancing about the room, he noticed that many of them avoided his gaze. He realized that he had no idea what he looked like. He could be old and hideous for all he knew. He spied a large brass mirror to one side of the room, as tall as a man. He walked to it slowly, continuing to try to make eye contact with the people he passed. As he reached the mirror, he tried to make it look at as though he was appreciating the handicraft and not looking at himself. As with all brass mirrors, the image reflecting back at him was distorted. There were dimples and waves in his reflection, and the color was a deep orange. But from what he observed, he was not old or ugly at all. He was perhaps in his late thirties with a broad nose and strong chin. He supposed the women were avoiding his gaze because they would prefer to not be saddled with a former warlord as a husband. He would have been considered a foreigner to the Han, and probably had a fierce reputation. He had mentioned considerable landholdings to the empress, but they were probably located some distance from the capital of Chang'an. He was probably not what most princesses would prefer in a husband. He wished he knew the warlord's name. It would be interesting to research this ancestor when he woke up.

Zhihao suddenly gasped. He watched as Jiayi passed behind him, her reflection clear in the mirror before him. He turned, and she was quickly lost in the crowd.

"Excuse me!" he said as he pushed his way in the direction she had gone, but he did not see her. He supposed it was possible that she was not really there. A figment of his dream and imagination.

"Did you see Lady Meirong just now?" he heard a voice ask. He turned and saw two men laughing with each other.

"How could you miss her?" the other man asked. "The prettiest of the empress's ladies. And I suppose quite a polo rider in bed as well."

The men laughed again, slapping each other on the back as they both tossed back cups of alcohol.

Meirong! That was the name of the woman his ancestor had married. Of course, it made perfect sense that he would dream of Jiayi as Meirong.

Zhihao walked over to the men and cleared his throat. "Where is Meirong?" he asked, and he thought the men cowered a bit at him.

"She...she went that way," one of the men said with a stutter, gesturing to a hallway.

"Much obliged," Zhihao said. Apparently he inspired as much fear in men as he did in women. He couldn't help but smile to himself a little at that.

He went to the hall, but he did not see Jiayi. He followed it to the end, grateful that the din of the party had died down a bit. He heard voices coming from the left. Jiayi was not alone. He inched to the edge and peeked around the corner. As in his dream previously, Jiayi was with Prince Junjie, and he had his arms around her.

"I have missed you so much," she simpered.

"I cannot stay long," Junjie said. "The empress will want me to speak with that warlord."

So, Lady Meirong was having an affair with Prince Junjie. Though, considering how good-looking the prince was known to be, Zhihao would not be surprised if the prince had many lovers.

"I understand," she said. "But I am still determined to help you. I won't let anything happen to you."

Junjie ran his hands over her hair. "You worry too much, my darling. I am strong. I am sure I can fight whatever is coming. I should never have unburdened myself to you."

"Do not apologize!" Jiayi said. "I will help you. I will save you. If I have to break the laws of heaven and earth to do it, I will!"

Zhihao started at her words. What a strange thing for Meirong to say.

"You are an incredible girl, Jiayi," Prince Junjie said.

"Jiayi?" Zhihao said. He was in such shock, he forgot he was supposed to be hiding.

Jiayi and Junjie looked at him, and Junjie drew his sword.

"Zhihao?" she asked. "What are you doing here?"

*Z*hihao woke with a start. The fire was nearly dead and he could hear the tweeting of birds. A maid jumped to her feet and lowered her head.

"I am sorry to disturb you, master," she said. "I only wanted to stoke the fire for you."

He looked around and realized he was still sitting in the chair, back in his own home. He had fallen asleep and had the strangest dream.

"It's fine," Zhihao said. "Continue with your work."

She bobbed a curtsey and went back to rebuilding the fire.

Zhihao got up from the chair and stretched. He saw that the sky was starting to lighten. He went to his room to dress. He would go to the university. He had missed too much work. He would leave instructions with his mother that any messages for him should be sent to the library immediately.

As he dressed, he tried to remember the details of the dream. It was funny how his historian's brain was trying to put together all the disparate pieces of the puzzle he was working on. The warlord. The bracelets. Jiayi. They all fit together somehow, but it would take him time to understand the complete picture. He would try to do some research on Meirong and Prince Junjie when he got to the library. Maybe he could find an image of Lady Meirong. If he was going to dream about her, it might be easier if he didn't see Jiayi's face.

Maybe I can change the past.

Jiayi's words hit him like a gust of wind and he collapsed onto his bed. He thought about the images she had drawn of Prince Junjie. Her sketches were always well done, but even the first drawing he saw of Junjie, he knew there was something special about it. The care she took with it. The way the prince seemed to be staring right back at the viewer. It wasn't just good—it was magnificent.

Jiayi had told Zhihao that she had met the prince before. Was it possible she had been meeting the prince in the body of Lady Meirong? What had she told the prince? *I will save you.* Jiayi had seemed disturbed when Zhihao told her that the prince had been murdered.

What if I can change the past?

She had not been speaking about correcting written history. She was speaking literally.

If I have to break the laws of heaven and earth to do it, I will!

Zhihao was such an idiot! He finally understood what was happening. That was why she didn't respond to his declarations of love. Of his desire to marry her. She didn't feel the same way about him. She was in love with Prince Junjie.

And she was going to change the past to save him.

FIFTEEN

*W*aiting for the prince made Jiayi nervous. She didn't know what he was going to try to do or if he would be successful. She wanted to trust him, but she didn't really know him. He had only offered to help her, and had never asked for anything in return, but he seemed to take for granted that she was his path to the throne. But after her inability to see anything in the items collected by the empress, Jiayi was worried about what the empress was going to do next.

She recalled her plan to sell the items she had stolen from the empress over the years and hide the money at the library. It was more imperative than ever that she have some way to protect herself should the empress expel her from the palace.

She peeked out the door of her room and saw that no one was standing guard. She dressed in her dullest outfit and lifted the floorboard that hid her treasures. She debated which ones and how many to take with her. She needed to sell them all as quickly as possible, but she did not want to draw attention to herself. The woman had told her which markets to visit to sell the different items, but she didn't think she could be away from the palace that long. The woman she had sold the jade to seemed helpful enough. Maybe she would be willing to buy everything Jiayi had. Jiayi knew that she could get more money if she went to the different markets herself, but she did not think she had that much time. She took about half of the items, including anything made of jade. Her hand hovered over Lady Meirong's necklace. No, she could never sell that. It was her only connection to Prince Junjie.

She replaced the floor panel and hid the items in her undergarment. Quickly and quietly, Jiayi rushed to the west gate.

"Where are you going?" one of the guards asked her.

"I have to run an errand for Her Majesty," Jiayi said. "You know I have permission."

The guards did know that she and Zhihao were allowed to work on the empress's special projects together. But they never seemed to tire of teasing her and trying to take advantage of her every time she went out.

"We will have to check you to make sure you aren't stealing," one of the guards said as he ran his tongue over his lips. She knew this man well, and hated him. He was one of the worst at abusing his position with the palace maids. As much as she hated the way the eunuchs extorted everyone in the palace for money, at least they did not abuse the maids' bodies. The guards were not cut like eunuchs, and only guarded the palace from the outside at night. But daylight did not seem to deter them from taking advantage of the many women within the palace walls. But Jiayi had prepared for this possibility.

"I am in a terrible hurry," Jiayi said, stepping close to

him. "Perhaps I could bring you something back when I return."

"Like what?" the man asked, amused. There was very little a maid could ever offer a guard that didn't involve the girl's humiliation.

"The name of a flower girl who will spend the evening with you," Jiayi said. "Paid in advance."

The two guards laughed and punched each other in the shoulder.

"You'll buy me a night with a flower girl?" the guard asked. "Wouldn't it be cheaper to just let me run my hands over you real quick?"

"Cheaper," Jiayi said, "but not faster. The flower girl will go as slowly as you like."

The man tried to hesitate, perhaps wondering if he could get more out of the bargain, but he was clearly excited at the proposition.

"Fine," he said, opening the gate. "Go on. But you better make sure she's good looking."

"I will," Jiayi said, and she rushed out to the street without looking back. She wondered how many more times she would be able to get away with that. If she tried it too often, they would know she was up to something. She needed to find a better way to get the jewels out of the Forbidden City.

But she couldn't worry about that right now. She needed to sell what she had and then hide it away in the library. But if Hu Xiaosheng or Zhihao were there, she wouldn't be able to do that. She didn't want anyone to know about her hidden money. It was the only thing she had that could ensure her future should the worst happen.

She did her best not to run to the market. She didn't want anyone to take note of her. As she arrived at the market, she walked slowly, pretending she was shopping. It could look strange if she went directly to the same shop she had visited before.

When she spied the shop, she saw that the woman was busy with a customer. The woman saw her and gave a small nod that she would be with Jiayi in a moment, so Jiayi lingered at another shop, pretending to be interested in some silks while she waited. She glanced back down the road to make sure the guards had not followed her. When she was satisfied they had not, she was about to turn back to the stall when she saw someone she did recognize. She gasped and stepped deeper into the booth.

The man in the white suit.

When Zhihao's old university associate Marcus tried to force her aboard his ship, there had been a Chinese man in a white suit at the top of the gangplank. She couldn't believe a fellow Chinese would be involved in kidnapping and selling women. She had no idea who he was, but he looked important. Powerful. And she knew he was dangerous. Whether or not he would know her by a passing glance, she had no idea. She could have just been any other woman to him. But she would never forget his face.

"The pattern on this one is particularly lovely in the light," the shopkeeper said as she tried to usher Jiayi out of the stall where the lighting was better.

"Oh!" Jiayi said, blocking the woman's path and keeping her back to the street. "I can see how unique it is already." She kept her voice low even though she probably didn't need to. She had not been close enough to the man for him to hear her voice.

"And such a good price," the woman went on. Jiayi nodded and smiled, but it did not reach her eyes. She realized she had trapped herself in this spot. She couldn't see if the man had passed by or was taking his time examining the many things for sale. Was he gone? Or would she have to wait hours for him to complete his business? At some point, she would have to take a chance and glance back out at the street.

"How many would you like?" the woman asked, growing excited that she was about to make a big sale. Jiayi was not quite sure how to let her know that she wouldn't be buying anything but not anger the woman so much that she be pushed out into the street.

"I'm not sure," Jiayi said, keeping her voice low. "My mistress has such discerning taste—"

"There are no silks more discerning than mine!" the woman declared with a laugh. "If you bring these home to her, she is sure to be pleased."

"I am certain," Jiayi said. She turned her head just slightly, trying to see back out into the street without stepping back, but she couldn't see anything.

"Tell you what," the woman went on, "if you buy four rolls, I'll give you a fifth one free just for you! You won't have to tell your mistress. It can be our little secret."

The woman was getting serious, and a little annoyed as she watched a couple of other possible customers pass by. Jiayi was taking far too much time with a woman she was not going to buy from.

"I will have to tell her what you showed me," Jiayi said. "Let her know that you are the best shop to buy from."

"If you don't buy today, I can't give you the free roll," the woman said, her voice rising in irritation. "How much did your mistress ask you to pay for the silk? I will see what I can do right now."

"I don't know," Jiayi said, running out of polite excuses.

"Then let me work," the woman said, pushing past Jiayi

to speak to another woman admiring the many colors of the soft silks.

Jiayi could not help but be shoved back into the street by the woman's forceful arms. She quickly glanced up and down the street, grateful she did not see the man in the white suit. But she nearly screamed when she felt a hand on her shoulder.

"Come, come," the jade seller said, beckoning Jiayi to follow her.

Jiayi sighed in relief when she realized it was just the helpful shopkeeper and not the man in the suit. She followed the shopkeeper, glad to soon be once again hidden in shadows.

"Another item so soon?" the shopkeeper asked, raising an eyebrow.

"My mistress is facing an arranged marriage to a very old man," Jiayi lied. "She needs money to escape."

The woman sighed and shook her head. "Many worse things in the world than an unhappy marriage. Would she rather be working in a flower house?"

"No," Jiayi said. "That is why she needs to sell the jewels her father has given her."

"I'll buy the jade," the woman said, holding out her hand. "But you'll have to go elsewhere to pedal the jewels."

"Please," Jiayi said, undoing one of the frog clasps of her *chaopao* and pulling the small package of items out. "I don't have that much time. Are you sure you cannot give me something for all of this?"

The woman opened the package and whimpered when she saw the items. Golden hairpins, jeweled brooches, embroidered kerchiefs, necklaces, rings, and more. Jiayi knew she had collected a vast hoard, and she was heartbroken to let everything go for a fraction of what they were worth. The woman would most likely give Jiayi only a small amount and then sell it for a fortune herself in the other markets.

The woman suddenly gripped Jiayi's arm. "Did you steal these?" she hissed, her voice low. "I don't want to lose my head for you."

"No!" Jiayi said. "My mistress gave them to me herself." A partial truth. The empress had given Jiayi the items to explore their past and then simply forgot to ask for them back. They were mostly items that had no memories, so they held little value to the empress.

"This is risky," the woman said, shaking her head as she picked through the various items. "Even for me, people will ask questions."

"Please," Jiayi said. "I—*she* desperately needs your help. Anything."

The woman looked up at Jiayi's slip of the tongue and sighed. She knew Jiayi was lying. But if she didn't want the items, she would have tossed Jiayi out the moment she saw the jewels. But fortunately for Jiayi, the woman's greed was winning out.

"Wait here." The woman went through a flap in the back of the stall into what were probably her living quarters. Jiayi shifted from foot to foot, worrying her lower lip, anxiously shifting her eyes up and down the road. The woman returned with a small silk purse that jingled as she handed it to Jiayi. "This is all the cash I have."

Jiayi opened the bag and took a quick count. It was more than she expected the woman to give her, but still much less than the jewels were worth. Jiayi nodded and handed the woman half of the jewels she had with her. The woman tisked her tongue and they haggled back and forth over which items were worth the money in the purse. Finally,

Jiayi parted with most of the jewels, but the largest pieces—a hair comb, a thick bracelet, and a ring—the woman refused to take.

"I wouldn't take them even if I had the money," she said. "They would attract too much attention for sure."

Jiayi understood and gratefully accepted the bag of coins and hid it and the jewelry she still had back in her *chaopao*. Maybe she should keep a few things back to sell later or in her new country anyway.

"Don't come back here," the woman said. "I don't need the trouble."

Jiayi was disappointed, but there was nothing she could do. She would have to find another buyer for the rest of her items. But for now, she would hide the money at the library. She thanked the woman once again and turned to leave the shop. But as she did, she found herself nose to chest with a tall man. When she looked up, she nearly screamed.

It was the man in the white suit.

"Excuse me," he said. "I didn't see you there."

Jiayi turned to run away, but she felt him grab her arm.

"I'm sorry," he said, a smile on his lips. "But do I know you? You seem familiar."

Jiayi felt a surge of panic. She kicked the man in the shin as hard as she could. He yelped and let go of her arm. She bolted away from him, down the road, dodging people and items and animals.

"Wait!" she heard him call, but she didn't stop, and she didn't dare look back.

She clutched at the items and coins hidden in her robe to make sure they were secure, and she kept running. When she got to the edge of the road, she turned right, then she took the next left. She zigged and zagged through the narrow alleys of the city's *hutongs* until she was out of breath. She stopped and bent over, putting her hands on her knees as she caught her breath. As she looked around, she realized she had no idea where she was. She had never been here before, and one *hutong* pretty much looked like any other. Rows and rows of grey slab houses crammed together so tightly you could not tell where one home ended and another began. Jiayi had grown up in a *hutong* just like this, but in a very different part of the city.

Jiayi ran her hands over her arms to calm her nerves. She was still shaking from her run-in with the man in the white suit. He wasn't wearing a white suit now, but she still knew it was him.

And he had recognized her. He might even know who she was. Marcus knew that she was somehow connected to Zhihao. If the man in the white suit wanted to find her, he would only need to go to Zhihao. That meant she couldn't go to the library right now. Maybe not ever again.

Jiayi looked one way, and then another. She was completely lost and had no idea which way to go. The alleys here were too narrow for even a rickshaw to travel down, so she couldn't find a driver to take her back to a more familiar place. She didn't want to waste her money on a rickshaw anyway.

"Lost?" a woman asked from behind her.

Jiayi whirled around and saw a young woman with a babe at her breast. "A little," she said. "I just need to go back to the marketplace."

The woman looked her up and down and then gave a curt nod. "Just back the way you came," she said. "Turn right at the end and keep walking straight. Can't miss it."

Jiayi felt the hairs on her arms and the back of her neck prickle, but politeness forced her to smile and thank the woman for her assistance. She went the way the woman suggested, but she kept glancing back over her shoulder wearily. She took a few deep breaths to calm her racing heart and looked up at the sun shining brightly overhead. Surely no harm would come to her in the middle of the day, but she needed to find her way back to the market before the sun began to set. She would have to worry about what to do with her bag of coins later. When she reached the end of the alley, there were only more narrow paths to her right and left. The woman had told her to go right, but for some reason, she didn't trust her. She glanced behind her, and when she didn't see the woman, she went left instead. She had not taken more than a step when she felt a rough hand on her arm.

"Wrong way, little sister," a man said with a laugh.

Jiayi tried to pull away, but he was too strong. She kicked, but he jumped back.

"Feisty," the man said as he grabbed her other wrist. "The boys will like that."

She screamed but could do nothing as he dragged her around a corner and toward a flower house, the women standing outside it laughing as she fought.

SIXTEEN

Zhihao shook himself out of his daze and finished dressing. He then rushed out of the house without eating, much to the consternation of his mother, jumping into the nearest rickshaw and heading to the library.

What if I can change the past?

Zhihao chuckled and ran his hand over his mouth. All this time he had been wondering if Jiayi could actually change the past. Right wrongs. Save lives. And she had been working on doing exactly that. He wondered if Hu Xiaosheng knew. Hu Xiaosheng had been training her to make her powers stronger. Give her more control over her visions. But did he have any idea what she was truly capable of? Zhihao doubted it. He had to assume at this point that there was quite a lot that Jiayi was keeping from him—and perhaps not just regarding her powers. She had been so fiercely defensive of Prince Kang. Was she hiding something there too? It was possible. He hated to think that he couldn't trust Jiayi, but right now, he didn't know what to think about her.

Did he even really love her?

If he didn't know her, how could he? Was he falling in love with a fiction? A person Jiayi had fabricated?

He groaned and rubbed his eyes. No, that wasn't possible. He'd been down this road before...many times. When he first met her, he didn't believe she could see the past. It took a long time for him to accept her powers as real. And he had never known her to lie or deceive him before. He didn't just love her. They were friends. Partners. If he could trust anyone, it would be Jiayi. She had once told him that she had secrets. That all people have secrets. Keeping one part of her life private was not the same as lying. Perhaps she didn't quite trust him as much as he thought. After all, only a few days ago, he had been violent with her. Then he turned around and asked her to be his wife. He shook his head at the absurdity of it. She was right to be cautious around him. To keep some parts of her life hidden.

As he jumped out of the rickshaw at the library, some of the fire that had possessed him before had diminished, and his legs felt heavy as he climbed the stairs. He had planned on doing research on Meirong and the warlord. But now, he wondered if he should focus on Prince Junjie. It would undoubtedly endear Jiayi to him if he were able to help her save the prince's life. But if he did, would he lose her forever? Even though the prince only existed in her visions, her visions were real to her. Her love for the prince must be real too. If the prince didn't die, but kept living, there would be nothing to stop her from continuing to see him. Even though they could never truly be together, how could Zhihao ever compete with a ghost? Jiayi could never love Zhihao the way she did Junjie.

Zhihao supposed he was getting ahead of himself. He had no idea if Jiayi even could help Junjie. Her question had been "what if." It was possible she couldn't do anything. And even if she could, she knew that any life with Junjie would be a fantasy. She wouldn't really choose a dream over a real man. Would she? He wasn't sure he wanted to know the answer to that.

"There is a weight upon you," Hu Xiaosheng said as Zhihao approached him.

"I haven't been sleeping well," Zhihao said.

"Jiayi's dreams are special because they happen while she is awake," Hu Xiaosheng said. "But even dreams of the night can hold great meaning."

Zhihao nodded. "I think my dreams, or my mind at least, are trying to tell me something. Help me work out answers I can't quite figure out on my own."

"What is the question?" Hu Xiaosheng asked.

Zhihao paused for a moment. There were so many, he didn't know where to begin. But he had to start somewhere. If he could only answer one question, what would it be?

"What happened to Prince Junjie?"

Hu Xiaosheng nodded, stroking his long beard. "Not the question I expected you to ask," he said.

"I surprised myself as well," Zhihao said. "But that is the only question I can clearly put into words. Finding out the truth about Junjie will make Jiayi happy. She is the only thing that matters."

"What does Prince Junjie have to do with Jiayi?" Hu Xiaosheng asked.

So, he didn't know about Jiayi's plan, Zhihao realized. Well, it was not his place to tell him.

"She has met him before, in her visions," he said. "She just wants to know more."

Hu Xiaosheng nodded and pressed his lips. He seemed to think there was more to the story, but he didn't ask. He stood up and leaned on his cane as he walked through the library and up the stairs to the second floor.

"In truth, it might not be possible for us to know what happened to Prince Junjie," Hu Xiaosheng said as Zhihao followed him. "The Forbidden City is full of records that we cannot access. What we have here is just a small part of what a few learned men have recorded and were preserved mostly through sheer accident."

Zhihao nodded. While most educated people devoted themselves to writing poetry or philosophy, very few bothered recording day to day lives or even significant events who were not ordered by the throne to do so. And records were often lost over time. Paper or linen or whatever people might write on easily dissolves. Stone tablets are broken. Language changes. Characters today hardly resemble the characters of hundreds of years ago. It was doubtful that Zhihao would be able to find a definitive answer to what happened to Prince Junjie, especially outside the palace. And as Jiayi had demonstrated, recorded history was often wrong.

But Hu Xiaosheng must have thought something of use was here. He began wandering up and down the aisles, mumbling to himself, trying to recall a specific memory that would lead to the answer.

"Prince Junjie," Hu Xiaosheng said, "was famous for his beauty. But he was far more than that."

"He was a general," Zhihao said. "A popular military leader."

"Perhaps," Hu Xiaosheng said. "But there are no records of him winning any decisive battles. Empress Wu's reign was marked by turmoil within her family. But the country was mostly peaceful. Some warlords wanted power for themselves, but even they were placated with a few well-arranged marriages."

Zhihao tensed at that. He needed to learn more about his ancestor who married Meirong. But that would have to wait for now.

"So, if he wasn't a particularly brilliant military man," Zhihao asked, "what was he known for?"

"He was a threat to Empress Wu's son, Emperor Zhongzong," Hu Xiaosheng explained. He then found whatever scroll he was looking for, pulling it down and handing it to Zhihao.

"But Zhongzong deposed his mother," Zhihao said. "He proclaimed himself emperor after imprisoning her."

He followed Hu Xiaosheng over to a long table and unfurled the scroll. "But if Zhongzong died or was imprisoned or banished, guess who could have inherited the throne," Hu Xiaosheng said.

Zhihao looked down at the family tree of the Tang Dynasty rulers. It took a moment for his eyes and mind to adjust to the archaic characters, but once they did, the names and dates began to form a picture.

"Junjie was the grandson of Wu's brother," Zhihao said. "Distant enough to not be a threat to succession if Empress Wu had enough sons and grandsons of her own."

"But she didn't," Hu Xiaosheng said. "Most of her sons died under mysterious circumstances."

Zhihao chuckled. "Much like Junjie himself would. Even today, many people think that she killed her own children to ensure her hold on the throne."

"But here is the very interesting part," Hu Xiaosheng said. He drew his finger across the scroll, to the family of Empress Wu's husbands, the emperors Taizong and

Gaozong. "This woman, Lady Meirong, she and the prince were lovers."

Zhihao's heart seized at the mention of Meirong. His ancestress.

"She was a niece of Gaozong," Hu Xiaosheng said. "While Junjie did not have a strong claim to the throne, she did. She was the granddaughter of an emperor and was no blood relation to Wu. Many people would have preferred a son of Meirong on the throne to the son of Wu. If Junjie had married Meirong, and the two of them had a son, their claim to the throne would be the strongest if something had suddenly happened to Zhongzong. Or their supporters could have simply deposed Zhongzong in favor of Meirong's son if they accumulated enough power."

"But Meirong," Zhihao said, his throat feeling so tight he was afraid his words were not making sense, "she married someone else. A warlord."

"How did you know that?" Hu Xiaosheng asked.

"Umm...it's right there," he said, pointing to the line from Lady Meirong to her husband, a man named Shidu. Shidu must have been the warlord ancestor.

Hu Xiaosheng hmphed. "Yes, but she only married him after Junjie's death."

"You think Meirong and Junjie were planning to marry in secret?" Zhihao asked. "Without the empress's blessing?"

"It would have been foolish, but people have risked far more for a chance at the throne," Hu Xiaosheng said.

"So, you think that Zhongzong might have killed Junjie as a...a preventative measure," Zhihao said.

"It is the most plausible theory," Hu Xiaosheng said. "But it could have been someone else. It could have been Empress Wu. Or Shidu. Or anyone else who had a reason to keel Junjie and Meirong apart. But whoever it was, we still don't know how or when Junjie was killed."

"But I know who can find out," Zhihao said.

"To what end?" Hu Xiaosheng asked, suddenly skeptical. "This has nothing to do with your work."

"I'm not sure yet," Zhihao said. "It will be up to Jiayi what to do with the information."

"Why is this important to her?" he asked, and Zhihao felt his face go hot. Hu Xiaosheng didn't know about Jiayi and Junjie, or her desire to change the past. But Zhihao wasn't sure if he should tell the old teacher or not. He suddenly felt embarrassed at the idea that he and Jiayi were wanting to change the past. It seemed like something Hu Xiaosheng would not approve of.

"Umm...well...she..."

"Hello?"

Zhihao was saved from having to explain by an unfamiliar voice calling out downstairs. "I should check..." he started to say, but he didn't bother finishing the sentence as he rushed back to the stairs. As he went back toward the entrance, he saw a man calling to someone through the open door.

"This is it!" the man was saying.

"Can I help you?" Zhihao asked, but as he got a better look at the man, he stopped in his tracks. He was wearing a perfectly tailored English suit. His hair was cut short. Even his cue was gone! And he held a bowler hat in his hands.

"Sorry about that," the man said, slicking his hand back over his sleek hair. "My wife is hopelessly lost. I'm looking for Long Zhihao." The man then held his hand out for a shake.

Zhihao hesitated before taking the man's hand. He was

clearly not from around here. "Why would you be looking for Zhihao?" he asked cautiously.

"Actually, it's my wife who is looking for him," the man said.

Zhihao felt his heart go cold. "Your...wife?"

The door to the library opened, and like a vision, Rebecca, her golden hair shining and her lips painted an enticing red, stood before him.

"Hello, Theodore," she said.

Zhihao's knees gave out and he stumbled to the floor.

SEVENTEEN

*J*iayi struggled as the man dragged her toward the flower house. What was worse was the squealing laughter of the other women—the flowers—who already worked there. Scantily clad and faces painted, the women did nothing to help Jiayi from the terrors within the brothel's walls, but seemed to take a perverted delight in the suffering that would come to her.

"This one has spirit," the man holding her said.

"She'll scream for you!" one of the women said, and they all laughed again.

Jiayi called upon the strength of the women from her visions, the pirates, the martial artists, the farm workers, the women of fortitude, to help her. She dug her feet into the muddy ground and lowered herself as much as she could, causing the man to stumble over her, releasing his grip on one of her arms. She stood up, twisting around behind the man, taking his arm with her, and in an instant, she had the advantage. He groaned as she twisted his arm behind him and kicked him in the back of one of his knees.

"You bitch!" the man grunted, but Jiayi only twisted further, pulling his arm up behind him.

"If I move your arm any farther, your shoulder will snap," Jiayi said with a voice she was not sure was her own.

The women had stopped laughing, but were staring in shock, glancing at one another with their hands over their mouths.

"If you want to escape, now is your chance," Jiayi said to them.

Most of the women ran inside the brothel, but two of them fled down the *hutong* alleys and did not look back. Jiayi watched until the girls were out of sight.

"You'll pay for that," the man grunted.

"Send the bill to the empress," Jiayi said. "Along with your doctor's fee." She then gave his arm the last twist it needed to pop his arm out of the socket. The man screamed and fell to the ground. Jiayi released him and turned to run away herself, but she found herself facing the man in the white suit.

"You are the girl from the dock," the man said.

Jiayi pulled her hands in front of her and assumed a fighting stance. "Will you be next?" she asked.

The man laughed. "Come," he said. "Let us leave this filthy place. We have business to discuss."

Jiayi was not interested in what this slave trader had to say, but she couldn't stay here in the *hutong* either. People had gathered around the flower house to find out what happened, and eventually, the man she had injured would gather his wits enough to send someone after her if she didn't get away.

"Let's go," she said, brushing past him, even though she still didn't know her way back to the road.

The man chuckled and quickly caught up with her. "My

name is Lian. What should I call you? You never did give Marcus your name."

"I'd rather keep that to myself for now," she said.

"Beautiful, dangerous, and smart," Lian said as the main road finally came into view, eliciting a sigh of relief from Jiayi. "I could use a woman like you."

"Save your flattery," Jiayi said. "I'll never work with a man like you."

"What do you know about me?" he asked.

"You sell women as slaves," Jiayi said. "That's enough for me to stay away from you. I should have you arrested."

Lian stumbled, surprised by her words, but Jiayi kept her head up and walked surely. Lian caught up with her.

"It isn't cheap, overthrowing an empire," he said. If he was hoping to shock her, he succeeded. Who would say such a treasonous thing to a complete stranger? But Jiayi did her best to hide her surprise.

"You are a revolutionary, then," Jiayi said.

"Aren't we all?" he asked with a wry smile.

"No," Jiayi said. She genuinely did not care who was on the throne. She only wanted her freedom. They made it to the main road, and Jiayi was about to run away again, leaving Lian far behind her, when he hailed a rickshaw.

"Come," he said, offering her his hand. "At least hear me out."

"How can I trust you?" she asked.

"You can't," he said. "But I guarantee you are going to want to hear what I have to say. And I'm fairly certain your curiosity is going to force you to get into this rickshaw with me."

Jiayi hated how right he was. Still, she hesitated, crossing her arms in front of her. It unnerved her how much he knew about her when he didn't know her at all. But she couldn't stand on the street forever. She climbed into the rickshaw, ignoring Lian's proffered hand, and together they rode toward the university. She was a little nervous that they were going to the library. She wasn't sure she could face Zhihao and Lian together. She assumed that Lian was one of Zhihao's revolutionary friends he had spoken of. Did he know that Lian had been the man she saw on the ship? That he was an associate of Marcus? Surely not. Zhihao would never condone slavery.

The rickshaw stopped a little ways from the university, in an upscale shopping and restaurant area. Jiayi, in her maid disguise, her feet muddy and her hair falling out of its plait, felt all the confidence of a few minutes ago rush out of her and she wanted nothing more than the earth to swallow her whole.

Lian seemed to sense her unease and offered her his easy smile and his hand. "Come," he said. "No one will care what you look like."

The glances directed her way by the men and women— Chinese and foreign—told her another story, but she had come this far. No sense in running away just yet. She took his hand and climbed out of the rickshaw. Lian wrapped her hand around the crook of his arm and led her into a tea house.

This was not like any tea house Jiayi had ever visited before. It was as though she had stepped into one of her dreams. The tables, chairs, and cups and saucers were in the British style, and most of the guests were in Western dress, even the Chinese patrons. But the most shocking part of all was the waitresses were white! The waitress bowed to them and then led them to a small table with two seats. Even though Jiayi could speak some English, she was at a loss for words when the woman tried to take her order. Lian ordered for both of them, and the waitress bowed again before she left. Never in her life did Jiayi imagine that a white woman would bow to her!

"Finally," Lian said, "I've shocked you speechless."

"I've been to restaurants before," Jiayi said, stretching the truth a bit but at least finding her voice again. "Just not in Peking."

"You've traveled, then?" Lian asked.

"You could say that," Jiayi replied.

"So, you are the court historian Zhihao has been working with all these months," he said. "Jiayi."

Jiayi started for a moment. Was there nothing the man wouldn't lie about? "So, you do know my name. Why the ruse?"

"I did not want to startle you more than I already had," he said, then he changed the subject. "Zhihao thinks quite highly of you."

The waitress returned with a pot of hot tea, two handled cups with saucers, and a plate of sweet and savory foods. Jiayi was glad that she had seen women in her dreams using such cups so she knew how to hold them and not make a fool of herself trying to do something as simple as drink tea. Lian poured the tea for her, and she took the liberty of adding her own milk and sugar.

"I enjoy working with him," Jiayi said.

"I think it is more than that," Lian said. "There must be a reason he has been keeping you from me. I've been trying to meet with you for weeks."

"It is not within his power to make introductions for me," Jiayi said. "If you hadn't found me in the market, you'd have to go through the empress to arrange a meeting. I doubt you have connections that high."

Lian regarded her for a moment, and she couldn't help

but wonder if she misspoke. If her words contradicted something Zhihao had told him. But she looked straight at Lian, not wavering in her resolve. She wondered which woman from her dreams had restored her confidence.

Finally, Lian cleared his throat and took one of the sweet pastries from the plate between them. She had passed the test. "So, what were you doing in the market?" he asked.

"What do you want?" Jiayi asked, ignoring his question as she sipped the tea, which was surprisingly sweet. She did her best not to grimace. She didn't know how foreigners could drink their tea in such a way.

"What do you know of Prince Kang?" Lian asked.

"Too much," Jiayi said. "And all of you are fools if you think your plan is going to work."

"You don't think Kang can be emperor?"

"There is an emperor," Jiayi said. "You can't just pick a new emperor because you don't like the current one. That's not how a dynasty works."

"Don't worry about the emperor," Lian said. "We will take care of him."

Jiayi cocked an eyebrow, then she shook her head. "I never should have come here. If the empress finds out, we are all going to lose our heads."

"Not if you take care of her first," Lian said.

Jiayi blinked, not sure she heard him right.

"Yes," Lian said, as though he could read her thoughts. She supposed the shock must have registered on her face. "You are the only person, the only woman, who can get close enough to the empress to end her life who I can entrust with such a task."

Jiayi stood up and tried to leave, but Lian grabbed her hand. "Let me go," she hissed. "This is stupid. Dangerous. Suicide!"

"Just hear me out," he said, pulling her back toward her chair. She sat back down with a plop, but kept her feet firmly on the floor should she need to bolt from the room. "Yes, it is dangerous."

"And stupid," Jiayi reaffirmed.

"And stupid," he agreed. "But the rewards...can you imagine?"

"No," Jiayi said.

"That is because you are Manchu," he said. "You have to believe that things are this way because of the Mandate of Heaven. If the gods did not approve of the Qing Dynasty, they would have intervened by now, yes?"

Jiayi shrugged. She didn't have much faith in the gods.

"I know you know about the seal," Lian said. "The Manchu didn't have the Mandate of Heaven. They lost it. They should have been deposed long ago. That is why China suffers. The Manchu have been holding onto ruler-ship that is not theirs."

"The empress has the seal," Jiayi said. "I found it for her."

"Which is why you should be the person to end her miserable life," Lian said, his voice growing animated. "She thinks her rule is secure now. But you will be the one to take it from her when she least expects it."

"Why would I do that?" she asked. "As you said, I am Manchu. I secured her throne by finding the seal. I am in the empress's favor. Why would I risk that?"

"Because a new world order is coming whether you help us or not," Lian said. "Either you will kill the empress, ushering Kang to the throne more quickly, or she will stay in power until she dies, and Kang will be emperor anyway. But if you don't help us, we will know that you are not our friend. The Manchu will fall, you among them."

"Are you threatening me?" Jiayi asked, and part of her was afraid of this obviously deranged man. Even Kang would not speak of killing the empress.

"No," Lian said. "I am warning you. I am giving you an opportunity to help yourself and all of China. If you kill the empress, then you will be a heroine in the new world order. A woman of power and influence. A woman of wealth."

"I just want to be free," Jiayi said without thinking. She closed her mouth and nearly cursed to herself. But Lian only nodded.

"If you do this, I will give you enough money to go anywhere in the world you want," he said. "You will be free."

Her eyes nearly began to water at the thought. Even Kang did not promise her freedom. He had hinted that he could make her a consort, but life within the walls of the Forbidden City—even life as an empress—was nothing more than a cage to her. She wanted to leave this place. Leave China. As much as she hated to admit it to herself, Lian's offer was frighteningly appealing.

"Why not Kang?" she asked. "He is one of you. He is closer to the empress than I am. He could...dispatch her for you. Why risk your plan by speaking to me?"

"It is too risky for him," Lian said. "If something...unnatural happened to her, he is the first person who would come under suspicion. We need someone else on the inside we can trust."

"And you think that person is me?" she asked, almost laughing.

"That's what Kang thinks," Lian said, and Jiayi was not laughing anymore.

Is this what Kang meant? Is this why her powers seemed to have little importance to him? He didn't need her abilities to see the past to get him on the throne. He needed an assassin.

"Thank you for the tea," Jiayi said as she stood up. "I should leave. The empress will wonder where I am."

"Think about it," Lian said, staying seated. "If you want to reach out to me, talk to Kang."

Jiayi gave him a nod and then walked out of the tea house as slowly as she could, which was still nearly a run. She needed to get away. Go somewhere she could think. She wished she had someone she could talk to. She was near the library, but somehow, she didn't think Zhihao would be too pleased with the idea that she was thinking of becoming an assassin. Kang would want her to do it. Der Ling...Der Ling only cared about the dagger. Hu Xiaosheng would be appalled that she would even consider committing murder.

As usual, Jiayi was utterly alone.

EIGHTEEN

"Are you all right?" Rebecca asked, rushing to Zhihao's side.

Thankfully, he hadn't passed out, only gone weak in the knees. But as he looked up into Rebecca's blue eyes, eyes he never thought he would see again, he had to blink a few times to make sure he wasn't dreaming.

"How?" was all he could manage to say.

Rebecca laughed. "I guess you didn't get my letters."

The letters! Of course. She had written to tell him she was coming. He thought she had written in the hopes of striking up a relationship again and that if he ignored her, she would disappear from his life again. He never imagined she would show up here in Peking.

"Oh," he said, his senses returning to him and he pushed himself to his feet, dusting off the seat of his pants and straightening his cuffs. He decided lying was the best approach. "No, I'm sorry to say I didn't. The post here is notoriously unreliable."

"Well, no matter," Rebecca said, the smile never wavering from her face. "We are here now."

"We?" Zhihao asked, looking over at the Chinese man who had first caught his attention.

The man held his hand out to shake. "Wei Huiqing. China special envoy to Great Britain. Or you can call me Henry."

Zhihao shook Henry's hand. "It is nice to meet you," Zhihao said. "What brings you to Peking?"

"I'm here to report to Her Majesty on the current state of affairs between our two countries," Henry said. "She wants to know 'the truth,' she said. The things the official ambassador won't."

"Can you believe I'm going to meet the empress?" Rebecca said, brimming with excitement.

"You?" Zhihao said. "Why would you..." His voice died away when he remembered that Henry mentioned his wife. "You...you're married," he stammered, his mouth going dry. He suddenly felt weak again, but he steadied himself.

"Yes," Rebecca said, glancing down and showing a bit of apprehension for the first time since she arrived. "We married six months ago."

Rebecca was married. Married! How could she? She had said she would never love anyone else. But here she was, married, and parading her new husband around in front of Zhihao. Why? For spite? Just to hurt him for never writing to her. For leaving? For letting Eli—No! He couldn't even begin to think about what happened if he wanted to remain in control of his emotions and words.

Zhihao cleared his throat. "Congratulations."

"Thank you," Rebecca said softly. "I do hope you can find it in you to be happy for me. When I never heard from you again, I thought...I hoped that you had met someone else. Or that your family had made an advantageous arrangement for you. I only ever wanted for both of us to be happy…one way or another."

Zhihao softened toward her. How could he have ever thought ill of her intentions? She was still the kindest, most gentle woman he had ever met. And it wasn't as though she had married immediately after he left. Only six months? She had been alone for years. She deserved to finally find someone.

"Yes, well," Zhihao said. "There is…someone in my life. Not a wife, though. At least, not yet."

"Oh, I'm so glad," Rebecca said, the smile and joviality returning to her face.

"But what brings you here?" Zhihao asked. "To the library?"

"You, silly!" Rebecca said. "Henry is from Shanghai and I've never been to China before, so we don't know anyone in the city other than a few stuffy bureaucrats. And their wives have been less than inclined to have tea with me."

"I'm sure the ladies are just trying to avoid any discomfort since they don't speak English," he said.

"But I speak Chinese," Rebecca said, and Zhihao's jaw nearly dropped when he realized they had been speaking Chinese the whole time. "I didn't stop studying just because you left. And Henry has been such a patient teacher."

Zhihao felt a little flustered. He should have known that Rebecca would not abandon her Chinese studies. She was a linguist. Learning languages was her passion and profession.

"Well," Zhihao said, "I'm sure you will find some ladies to take tea with at the foreign legation."

"Indeed," she said. "We are staying at a hotel in the British Quarter. It's perfectly dreadful, as though we never left London."

Zhihao chuckled. He'd never been in the legation, but he'd heard much the same thing from other people who had.

"How long will you be in Peking?" Zhihao asked, his nerve calming enough to feign a normal conversation.

"A few weeks," Rebecca said. "Henry has to wait for the empress's summons. Apparently, we won't find out she has time to meet with him until the night before she is ready, which could be any time in the next month. But while I'm here, I'm on a bit of a business venture of my own."

"Oh?" Zhihao asked.

"The Metropolitan Museum of Art in New York City is finally curating a permanent Chinese exhibit," Rebecca explained. "I'm here on their behalf to purchase high-quality items of which the history can be confirmed."

"That's fantastic," Zhihao said. "I'm currently building a collection myself in the hopes of building a museum here in China to house and protect historical artifacts."

"What a happy coincidence," Henry said, clearly desperate for a chance to join in the conversation. "You must know the best places to take my wife shopping."

"Unfortunately," Rebecca said, "the history of items found in markets cannot usually be confirmed. But if you have any items that have been dug up, or purchased from families who know their history, I would be more than glad to talk business with you."

Zhihao suddenly felt a little uneasy. The whole purpose of his museum was to keep Chinese relics in China. Rebecca's mission smacked of the same hubris he saw in Marcus. While he did not doubt Rebecca's good intentions, he could not ignore the fact that her goals were in direct conflict with his own.

"What the bloody hell is taking so long!" a loud voice boomed, and Zhihao's stomach turned sour.

"What is he doing here?" Zhihao growled as Marcus burst through the library door.

"He's my business partner," Rebecca said.

"Are you mad?" Zhihao asked, not bothering to check his words before he spoke.

"What do you mean?" Rebecca said. "He is one of the leading suppliers of Chinese memorabilia in London. The Met paid a pretty penny for a partnership with him."

"Then the Met has even lower standards for their artifacts than the London Museum," Zhihao spat.

"Teddy, Teddy, Teddy," Marcus said, shaking his head. "This old argument? I thought that sexy little minx I met the last time I was here had put you in your place about that."

"I told you not to call me that," Zhihao said through gritted teeth.

"Marcus," Rebecca gasped. "You didn't tell me that you had seen Theodore in recent years."

"I didn't want to upset you given your...past," Marcus said. "But when you said you wanted to visit the library, I thought you were coming to check out a book. I didn't know Teddy was the librarian."

"I am not a librarian," Zhihao said, his nostrils flaring at this point, his arms crossed across his chest. "I'm a historian."

Marcus raised his eyes to look at the rows and rows of bookshelves. "You look like a librarian to me."

"Get out," Zhihao said, pointing toward the door. "You aren't welcome here."

"I think only librarians can order people out of a library," Marcus teased.

"Then I'm a librarian," Zhihao said. "If it gets you the hell out of here."

Marcus laughed as he opened the door. "Oh, Teddy. How I missed you. Maybe I'll call on your little friend instead."

Zhihao noticed that Marcus never said Jiayi's name. He wondered if Marcus didn't actually know who Jiayi really was. If he didn't, he didn't want to be the one to send Marcus in her direction, so he kept his mouth closed as Marcus finally walked out the door.

"What was that all about?" Rebecca asked.

"How can you work with him?" Zhihao asked, the disdain clear in his voice.

"This is a rare opportunity," she said. "I couldn't refuse."

"How could you compromise your morals like that?" Zhihao asked.

"What?" Rebecca asked, her eyes going wide. "I haven't—"

"Dear," Henry said, placing a hand on her arm. "Perhaps we should return to the hotel for now."

Rebecca exhaled through her nose. "Yes, dear," she said.

"We would love to speak to you further," Henry told Zhihao. "Perhaps dinner, tomorrow night?"

"Of course," Zhihao said. "Let me check my schedule and I'll contact you at your hotel."

Henry gave Zhihao a card for the hotel and ushered Rebecca out the door. But Rebecca stopped and turned back to Zhihao.

"And do bring your special lady with you," she said. "I can't wait to meet her."

"She would love it," he said even though he really had no idea how Jiayi would feel about meeting Rebecca in person.

Rebecca gave him a smile and nod and left the library, her husband on her heels. Zhihao watched the door as it slowly closed behind them, trying to make sense of what just happened.

He never thought he would see Rebecca again. Now that he had, his heart was racing. It was as if he didn't care that she was married. She was the same beautiful, smart, happy girl he used to know. Back from before everything went wrong. He knew that he had never stopped loving her. They were both in a dark place after Eli's death. They were hurting, and they often lashed out at each other. So, when Zhihao finished his program a few months later, he left England. He told Rebecca goodbye, but it hadn't felt final. It was as though they simply needed some time and distance but would find each other again. But they didn't. Once Zhihao stepped off the boat back in Peking, he closed the door on that part of his life, never to open it again.

Or so he thought.

He turned around and nearly jumped out of his skin when he saw Hu Xiaosheng standing there.

"Why didn't you introduce me?" Hu Xiaosheng asked.

"How long have you been standing there?" Zhihao asked.

"Long enough," Hu Xiaosheng said as he made his way back to his table and eased onto his stool.

"For what?" Zhihao asked, following him.

"To see you go from being determined in your endeavors to questioning everything you thought you believed," Hu Xiaosheng said. "One smile from that woman, and you forgot Jiayi even existed."

"That's...not exactly true," Zhihao said. "I told Rebecca that there was a woman in my life. I was talking about Jiayi."

"You fell over when you saw that woman!" Hu Xiaosheng yelled. He never raised his voice. "When did you ever trip over yourself for Jiayi?"

"I was in shock," Zhihao said. "Did you ever expect to see a woman like that walk in here."

"Bah!" Hu Xiaosheng said, waving Zhihao off. "Jiayi was a thousand times more radiant the first time she walked in here. You should trip over yourself every time you see that girl and thank the celestial beings she even speaks to you!" He then turned back to his table and flipped open a book so hard it immediately bounced back closed. He grumbled and fussed with the book to try and find the page he wanted, but he just settled on a page at random and began mumbling to himself.

Zhihao couldn't help but find it endearing how protective the old man was of Jiayi. But he knew he was right. He was lucky to have Jiayi in his life. But he had also acted like a fool when he saw Rebecca. He could certainly chalk up his initial response to shock, but the next time he saw her, he would have to control himself.

Rebecca was his past. She was married. She was going to work at a museum in America. There was no reason for Zhihao to lose his faculties in her presence. It was clear that she only wanted to be friends. They had a lot of history together and she was lonely here in the city.

But Jiayi, she was his future. He just had to make sure she knew that too.

NINETEEN

*A*s Jiayi rode back to the Forbidden City, her mind was whirling. She almost could not believe what had just happened. That man, Lian, had really asked her to kill the empress. Was he crazy? She could hardly kill a bug, much less a human being. Especially someone as powerful as the empress. It would be impossible for her to get away with it. She would surely be caught and executed. The Minister of Justice would probably reinstate the Death by a Thousand Cuts just for her for doing something so wicked. Besides, what had the empress ever done to her to deserve such a fate? The empress was cruel, yes, but Jiayi knew that life on the streets could be much worse. Even today, she had almost been dragged into a flower house where she would have been raped and locked in a room to be sold over and over again until she accepted and submitted to her new life. Life as a palace slave was still preferable to the life she would have had if she had remained in poverty with her mother and sisters.

For a moment, her mind dared to wonder what had

happened to her family. She nearly opened her mouth to tell the driver to take her back to the old *hutong* where she was raised. But she stopped herself. There was no point in it. By now, her family had likely moved on. Dove, who was only two years younger, was most likely married. Little Pheasant, well, it would be a miracle if she survived childhood at all. And Mama...Jiayi could not even guess. She could have remarried. Had more children. It was more likely she was dead, though. And if her family were alive, what could she do for them? She couldn't even help herself. How could she help a whole family?

Jiayi sat back in the rickshaw and waited for it to deliver her back to her walled cage. She knew that Lian was a dangerous man. She would have to do her best to avoid him. She should also warn Zhihao about him.

She clutched the small purse of coins and the few trinkets she still had hidden in her robe near her chest. She didn't take them to be hidden at the library. She would have to secret them back to her room until another day. It was getting late, and if the empress had not already noted her absence, she surely would soon.

The rickshaw pulled to a stop outside the Forbidden City. She gave him a coin for his service and walked toward the western gate. As the gate opened, her heart froze in her chest when she saw the guard standing there, licking his lips eagerly for the name of the flower girl he thought he would be spending the evening with. She had completely forgotten. She stopped walking and quickly turned in the other direction to run.

"Hey!" the guard called as he ran after her. He was much faster than she would have thought possible. He carried a long lance, which he stuck between her feet, causing her to tumble to the ground, banging her chin and scraping her palms.

"Got ya!" he yelled, grabbing her by the hair and dragging her to her feet. She struggled, but could not dislodge his hand from her hair without ripping the strands from her scalp.

"Let go!" she yelled. "The empress will be angry if you hurt me."

"The empress will be furious enough at you for sneaking out," he said with a laugh. They both knew that the empress could and would much more readily punish a member of the inner court than a guard.

"I guess you didn't find me a girl," the guard said. Jiayi didn't bother answering. She was too busy holding tightly to his wrist to lessen the pressure on her skull. "No matter. You'll do."

The guard took her inside the gate, and another guard slammed the door shut behind her. The guard took Jiayi behind a bush and shoved her to the ground, never releasing her hair. She was face-down, her mouth and nose in the dirt. She screamed for help, but the guard paid no mind. He pulled her robe up to her thighs, running his hands over her skin.

"I'm going to enjoy this," he said.

"Stop!" a commanding voice said.

The guard immediately released Jiayi and scurried out of the shrubbery like a frightened rat. He and the other guard kneeled before Princess Der Ling.

Jiayi pulled her robe down and ran to the princess, kneeling behind her.

"What is going on here?" Der Ling asked.

"Nothing, Your Highness," the guard said. "I caught this

maid sneaking out. I was just giving her a beating, teaching her a lesson."

"It looked like you were about to do a lot more than beat her," Der Ling said. "And it is not your place to punish maids anyway. I do not think the empress would be pleased to know that you were usurping her authority over her own household."

"No, my lady," he said. "Apologies. It won't happen again."

"You are right," she said. "It won't." Der Ling then jerked her head, and several other guards that Jiayi hadn't noticed rushed forward, grabbing the guard by his arms and taking him away.

"Your Highness!" the guard said, obviously shocked. "Please, I'll do anything you ask."

Der Ling shrugged. "You won't be able to do much when you are dead."

The other guard who had not stopped the man from trying to rape Jiayi was breathing quickly, terrified that he would be the next to face Der Ling's wrath. But instead, her voice softened toward him.

"I trust we will have no further issues," she said to him.

"No, Your Highness," the man said, never daring to raise his head.

"Good," she said, then she turned and walked away.

Jiayi got to her feet and shuffled silently behind the princess. She was both frightened and awestruck by the woman's ruthlessness. Usually, in a situation like that where someone found themselves in a position of blackmail over another, the person would use that ability to the full. Jiayi was shocked that Der Ling did not extract a promise from the man that he would never stop her from exiting the palace or something. But instead, the man would be severely punished for assaulting a member of the empress's household. He would be castrated, if he was allowed to live at all. But Jiayi also knew that the other guard, the man who had basically done nothing, would now fear Der Ling for the rest of his life. He would never stop her from doing whatever she wanted and would always do her bidding. Der Ling had eliminated an enemy and gained an ally. Jiayi could not help but be impressed.

Der Ling walked to her own palace, not saying a word as Jiayi followed behind.

"Get out," she said to her attendants once they were inside the palace, and the women and eunuchs quickly left, shutting the door behind them. Jiayi was on her knees before Der Ling, and she held her breath, waiting for the woman to speak.

"You are filthy," Der Ling said. "Why are you dressed like a peasant?"

"It's been a long day," Jiayi said with a sigh.

Der Ling reached into her sleeve and pulled out the silver bracelet, the one Jiayi had stolen from Empress Wu in a vision. She recoiled, and Der Ling noticed, raising an eyebrow.

"Why were you keeping this from me?" Der Ling asked.

"I don't know what you are talking about," Jiayi said. "Zhihao had it. He was going to get rid of it."

"Why?"

Jiayi hesitated. If Der Ling knew it was connected to Empress Wu, she would either want Jiayi to touch it or she would give it to the empress, who would force her to touch it.

"When I touched it, the vision was terrifying," Jiayi said.

"A young woman being executed." She couldn't stop tears from filling her eyes at the memory. "I thought I was going to die. If I hadn't woken up when I did..." Her voice broke and she slapped her hand to her mouth.

"But why did you want to keep it from me personally?" Der Ling asked, pulling out and unfolding the piece of paper with her name on it. "I thought we were friends. That we were working together."

"I don't know why Zhihao wrote that," Jiayi said, getting a better look at it. *Der Ling has the bracelet*, it said. "All I can imagine is that he was trying to warn me because he knew it was dangerous for me. And he was right. You made me touch it! If I hadn't been so exhausted, you could have killed me if I had returned to that same vision."

For the first time, Der Ling's mask cracked and she looked afraid. But she quickly cleared her throat, and her face once again betrayed no emotion. "I am sorry," she said. "I had no idea that you believed you could die in a vision."

"They are just as real to me as my waking life," Jiayi said.

Der Ling tossed the bracelet aside. "Well, if you are that afraid of it, I'll get rid of it."

"You will?" Jiayi asked, surprised.

"Of course," Der Ling said. "We are friends. I would never do anything to endanger your life."

"Thank you," Jiayi said.

Der Ling chuckled. "Why do you seem so surprised?"

"I...I have never had a real friend," Jiayi said.

"What about Zhihao?" Der Ling asked, and Jiayi shrugged. Der Ling laughed. "Who can ever understand men, right?"

Jiayi allowed herself a small laugh and nodded in agreement.

"Forget about Zhihao," Der Ling said as she crossed the

room to a chest that was locked. She pulled a key out of one of her sleeves and unlocked it, revealing Empress Wu's dagger. "Forget the empress. Forget Kang." She walked over to Jiayi and offered her the dagger.

Jiayi pulled her sleeves over her hands and took the dagger. Even through the fabric, she could feel heat. Energy. Electricity sparking at the tips of her fingers. The dagger, like the bracelet, was calling to her. It needed to show her something.

"Will you touch the dagger for me, Jiayi?" Der Ling asked. "Tell me what secrets it holds."

Jiayi flipped one of her sleeves back and took a deep breath.

*J*iayi was surprised when she opened her eyes to see that she was still holding the dagger. The items that took her back in time were not always so obvious.

"What are you doing, Wu Mei?"

Jiayi looked up and saw an older woman dressed in the Tang style with an ornate headdress.

"What I should have done the moment I entered the palace, *Your Majesty*," Wu Mei, the young Empress Wu, said with contempt.

"You wouldn't dare," the older woman, who Jiayi thought must be Empress Wang, said. "Guards!"

"They aren't coming," Wu Mei said. "They don't love you. They won't protect you. You are old. You are worthless. Taizong loves me. He only ever loved me. With you out of the way, I will be empress and we can finally be happy."

Empress Wang laughed. "You always were a foolish

child. Being an empress is never about love. It is about duty. Honor. Things you know nothing about. One day, Taizong will realize that you might wear the crown of an empress, but you never learned to be more than just the spoiled child you were the first time you walked through the palace gates."

"Maybe," Wu Mei said. "But at least you will not be there to see it."

With that, Wu Mei thrust the dagger forward, piercing through the thick embroidered robes that Empress Wang wore, and slicing into her chest with shocking ease.

Jiayi cried out, but Wu Mei stopped her from screaming as the empress collapsed to her knees. Wu Mei pulled the dagger back, the steel red with blood. The empress clutched at her chest, but her face was already pale, her body going weak.

"I curse you, Wu Mei," the empress rasped, a trickle of blood seeping from the side of her mouth. "That dagger will be your doom. Taizong will despise you. Your children will betray you."

"This dagger was blessed by the gods," Wu Mei said. "Carved with sacred sigils and prayed over by the holiest of nuns at my convent. With you dead, I will be empress—and so much more."

With that, Wu Mei slashed the empress's throat, blood pouring forth and down the front of her gown. The old woman clutched at her neck as she gasped and sputtered, but there was nothing she could do as her life force poured out. She fell forward, the blood pooling around her.

Wu Mei stepped back and tisked her tongue. "She got blood on my shoes, the old bat." She then spat on the dead empress's body and returned the dagger to its sheath without bothering to wipe the blood from it.

When Jiayi opened her eyes, she no longer saw the dagger the same way. What were merely beautiful carvings before were now swirling symbols of ancient magical power. Power that felt like a million tiny bee stings on the palm of her hand.

Whether the dagger was truly magical, if it gave Wu Mei the power to become empress, or if it only gave Wu Mei the courage to do whatever it took to become empress, Jiayi wasn't sure. Either way, the dagger was not something to be trifled with.

"Well?" Der Ling asked when Jiayi did not say anything. "What did you see?"

Jiayi now knew the truth. Wu Mei had killed Empress Wang and took the throne for herself with the help of the dagger. While many people had always suspected Wu Mei of killing Empress Wang, there was no evidence. But Jiayi held the proof in her hand. Jiayi pulled the dagger from the sheath and examined it carefully. Around the very edge of the sheath's opening, there was a dark stain. The stain of murder. The stain of treachery. The stain of the empress's blood.

If Wu Mei used the dagger to kill Empress Wang and become empress herself, would Der Ling do the same thing? Could Prince Kang use it to kill the empress and his cousin, the young emperor, and set himself up as a new emperor?

And what about Lian's promise? If she killed the empress, he would make sure she was honored in the New China. Would he have the revolutionaries make her their new leader? Their new empress?

As absurd as it sounded, Jiayi had to believe that anything was possible.

Jiayi looked up at Der Ling. "I saw nothing."

THANK YOU FOR READING!

Jiayi and Zhihao will return in *The Slave's Necklace*!
Subscribe to my mailing list so you will be the first to find
out when it is released!
http://amandarobertswrites.com/subscribe-touching-time/

THE SLAVE'S NECKLACE

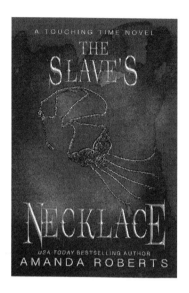

https://amzn.to/2Hw2IAQ

Kill the Empress, save China.

That is what people from all sides are telling Jiayi. She not only has the power to kill the empress, but to set up a new future for China. Jiayi has spent her life as a palace slave. Freedom for China could mean a lifetime of servitude for her.

And Jiayi is tired of living for everyone else.

As Jiayi's powers grow, she finds herself living more and more in the past, even as the future is barreling toward her.

Zhihao's past is catching up with him, leaving death and heartache in its wake. Zhihao is going to have to make a choice, but he isn't sure he can do it alone.

Jiayi and Zhihao stand on the precipice of a new world. But they will only survive if they can overcome the past and stand together, no matter how much it hurts.

Get lost in time in this thrilling conclusion to the Touching Time Trilogy!

THE MAN IN THE DRAGON MASK

http://amandarobertswrites.com/dragonmask/

One Face

Two Men

And A Secret That Could Destroy An Empire

At the dawn of the Ming Dynasty, the emperor will do anything to ensure the future of his empire. Building the Forbidden City in fulfillment of his father's dreams is only the beginning.

But few people share the emperor's vision.

When a consort's betrayal has devastating consequences that rock the imperial court, the emperor discovers that the fight for the dragon throne has only begun.

ABOUT THE AUTHOR

 Amanda Roberts is a USA Today best-selling author who has been living in China since 2010. She has an MA in English from the University of Central Missouri and has been published in magazines, newspapers, and anthologies around the world. Amanda can be found all over the Internet, but her home is Amanda-RobertsWrites.com.

Website: http://amandarobertswrites.com/

Newsletter: http://amandarobertswrites.com/subscribe-touching-time/

Facebook: https://www.facebook.com/AmandaRobertsWrites/

InstaGram: https://www.instagram.com/amandarobertswrites

Goodreads: https://www.goodreads.com/Amanda_Roberts

Amazon: http://amzn.to/2s9QzAG

BookBub: https://www.bookbub.com/authors/amanda-roberts-2bfe99dd-ea16-4614-a696-84116326dcd1

Email: amanda@amandarobertswrites.com

ABOUT THE PUBLISHER

VISIT OUR WEBSITE
TO SEE ALL OF OUR HIGH QUALITY BOOKS:

http://www.redempresspublishing.com

Quality trade paperbacks, downloads, audio books, and books in foreign languages in genres such as historical, romance, mystery, and fantasy.